"C'mon, Devon, confess," Enid said. "We know it was you who saved us. Don't bother with the false modesty."

He couldn't let this go on any longer. Devon had to tell them the truth . . . didn't he? He opened his mouth to tell Enid that she had the wrong guy, but then he caught a good look at Elizabeth's face.

She was smiling brightly and looked even more beautiful than the angelic image of her that haunted his dreams. In her lovely blue-green eyes there was nothing but pure admiration. And it was all for him—for the guy she believed had saved her.

Knowing he would regret it but unable to stop himself, Devon stepped forward and wrapped Enid in a hug. "I was glad to," he said.

After disentangling himself from Enid, Devon turned toward Elizabeth. She threw her arms around his neck. As he pulled her close, inhaling her clean, wonderful scent, he realized that he'd never before felt such warmth of love for a girl as he did in Elizabeth's embrace.

But then Devon shuddered.

Because Elizabeth's love was based on a lie.

Visit the Official Sweet Valley Web Site on the Internet at:

http://www.sweetvalley.com

SWEET VALLEY High®

AFTERSHOCK

Written by
Kate William

Created by
FRANCINE PASCAL

BANTAM BOOKS
NEW YORK · TORONTO · LONDON · SYDNEY · AUCKLAND

RL 6, age 12 and up

AFTERSHOCK

A Bantam Book / December 1998

Sweet Valley High® is a registered trademark of Francine Pascal.
Conceived by Francine Pascal.
Produced by 17th Street Productions,
a division of Daniel Weiss Associates, Inc.
33 West 17th Street
New York, NY 10011.
Cover photography by Michael Segal.

ISBN: 0-553-49236-5

Published simultaneously in the United States and Canada

Bantam Books are published by Bantam Books, a division of Bantam Doubleday Dell Publishing Group, Inc. Its trademark, consisting of the words "Bantam Books" and the portrayal of a rooster, is Registered in U.S. Patent and Trademark Office and in other countries. Marca Registrada. Bantam Books, 1540 Broadway, New York, New York 10036.

PRINTED IN THE UNITED STATES OF AMERICA

OPM   0 9 8 7 6 5 4 3 2

To Molly Jessica Wenk

AFTERSHOCK

Chapter 1

Jessica Wakefield's shoulder felt as if it were going to pop out of its socket.

Forcing herself to ignore the pain, Jessica stretched her arm even farther over the edge—down into the deep fissure the earthquake had split open in the ground. But still she couldn't reach the white-knuckled fingers of Alyssa Hewitt.

In any other circumstances Alyssa would have appeared to be a pretty twelve-year-old with curly red hair, but right now she didn't look pretty at all. The girl looked absolutely terrified, her chin shaking, her mouth gaping, her eyes wide with horror.

Of course she looks terrified, Jessica thought as she tried to give Alyssa a calm, reassuring smile. *I feel really close to screaming hysterically myself!* Alyssa was clinging to a small, thin ledge a few feet down the fissure. Below her dangling feet was nothing but sheer drop.

"Hold on," Jessica told the girl, gritting her teeth as she renewed her efforts to grasp Alyssa's fingers. "I'll get you out of there, I promise!"

But Alyssa's fingers were starting to slip. "Help!" she squealed. "Help me!"

"Hold *on!*" Jessica ordered Alyssa again.

Alyssa let out a tiny, shrill screech as one of her hands detached from the ledge.

"No!" Jessica screamed. She scooted forward on her stomach until her head and shoulders were over the edge, but Jessica couldn't reach Alyssa's remaining five clinging fingers.

Alyssa wailed again as her fingers slipped loose one by one. Four . . . three . . . two . . . For a split second just Alyssa's index finger held her from her death.

This isn't happening, Jessica thought wildly. *Something will save her! She can't die!*

But Alyssa's last finger let go. Her wide eyes bored directly into Jessica's, filled with horror and . . .

Understanding, Jessica thought. That was the worst part. Alyssa knew exactly what was happening to her. She was falling to her death.

As she plummeted, the little girl's huge eyes remained locked onto Jessica's. Alyssa shrieked in terror. The piercing sound ripped through Jessica like an eagle's talon.

Jessica screamed and screamed—until her lungs ran out of air.

Then she sat up in bed, covered in sweat.

It had been a dream. A nightmare. Jessica took a deep breath, trying to calm her frantic heartbeat. She stared out into the darkness of the room, feeling cold waves of despair wash over her. Of course she was having nightmares—after the earthquake Jessica feared she would never sleep in peace again.

Maybe . . . , Jessica thought with a spark of hope, *maybe if Alyssa was just a nightmare, then the whole earthquake never happened. Maybe it was* all *an incredibly awful dream!*

Jessica reached over to the nearby end table and fumbled around until she managed to find the switch on the lamp. As soon as she turned on the light, though, her tiny flicker of hope was extinguished.

She was in an ornate, opulent guest bedroom of Fowler Crest. The walls were paneled in rich mahogany, with antique brass fixtures. Across from the enormous canopy bed a giant smoky mirror covered nearly the whole wall. The carpet on the floor was the color of red wine. It was a beautiful room, but as she peered around Jessica felt misery settle in her stomach in a heavy lump. The earthquake had really happened, or she wouldn't be having nightmares in this deluxe feather bed. She'd be sleeping soundly in her own bed, in her own home.

But the Wakefields' house had been completely wrecked. And Mr. and Mrs. Fowler had kindly offered to let Jessica, her parents, and her twin sister, Elizabeth, stay at Fowler Crest until their house

3

could be rebuilt. Whenever that would be.

Jessica had to sniffle hard to avoid being overwhelmed by tears. The earthquake had struck during her seventeenth birthday party and had flattened most of Sweet Valley. Elizabeth and her best friend, Enid Rollins, had almost been killed by downed power lines in the Wakefield backyard. Olivia Davidson and Ronnie Edwards had both *died*. And despite how hard Jessica and Bryan, Alyssa's older brother, had tried to save the poor girl, there was no denying the horrible fact that Jessica had watched as Alyssa tumbled to her death.

As much as she wished it were all a bad dream, Jessica knew from the pain in her aching, bruised heart that all the horror had really happened. Jessica turned over onto her side, curling into a ball, racked with sorrow.

Worst of all was the guilt.

There must have been something I could've done to save Alyssa, Jessica told herself. *I didn't try hard enough! I failed, and now a girl is dead.*

Tears began to trail down Jessica's cheeks. At that moment what Jessica wanted to do was run into the guest bedroom where Elizabeth was sleeping and hug her sister until all the guilt and misery faded away. As much as she sometimes fought with her twin, Jessica realized that nobody could make her feel better than Elizabeth.

That was part of the special bond they shared, a bond that went deeper than their extremely different personalities. Even though Jessica and Elizabeth looked incredibly similar on the outside, with their shoulder-length golden hair, eyes the color of the Pacific Ocean, and trim, athletic figures, inside they were as unlike each other as sisters could be. Elizabeth was usually far more serious, which the twins chalked up to Elizabeth being four minutes older.

She's always taken care of me, Jessica thought. *I can count on her no matter what.* And Elizabeth always knew the right words to say. Best of all, she knew how to listen.

There was only one problem—Elizabeth had just been in a near fatal accident. After the earthquake Jessica had arrived at the ruined Wakefield house just as Elizabeth was regaining consciousness from her near-electrocution by downed power lines.

The memory seemed blurry as Jessica thought back, as though she were remembering it through gauze. Jessica had left Bryan Hewitt with two police officers after Alyssa had fallen to her death and had raced home to check on Elizabeth. But Jessica's senses had been numbed by shock. She vaguely recalled the tearful reunion with her parents, Elizabeth, and her brother, Steven, in the front yard, but most of her memories of that reunion seemed far away, almost as though they were happening to someone else. Even the joy of learning that Elizabeth would be OK had been muted by the misery Jessica had felt at being so much a part of Alyssa's terrible death.

Elizabeth had been taken to the hospital but quickly released—Joshua Fowler Memorial had been jam-packed with casualties from the earthquake, and Elizabeth's injuries had turned out to be minor. The doctor had just warned Elizabeth to get lots of rest in order to allow herself to recover properly.

Which was why Jessica couldn't bother her twin now. But she needed to talk to *someone*.

Jessica slid out of bed. Lila's bedroom was down the hall, at the opposite end from the guest suites. Although Jessica and Lila were best friends, they didn't really have the kind of relationship where they discussed their problems . . . not really personal problems anyway. Jessica's friendship with Lila was based more on shopping, talking about guys, and gossiping about their friends at school. But Jessica was desperate. She and Lila had been through a lot together. Maybe Lila would see how much Jessica needed her now.

The wooden hallway floor felt cool and slick under Jessica's bare feet. Dim, dark yellow lights behind the baseboards came on automatically as Jessica crept down the hall, illuminating her way.

When she reached Lila's room, Jessica eased open the door and slipped inside. Lila was snoring rhythmically and actually quite loudly. As Jessica got closer to Lila's vast sleigh bed she almost allowed herself a small smile—Lila looked messier than Jessica had ever seen her. With the help of a rectangle of bright moonlight that fell over the bed, Jessica could see that Lila's usually coifed long brown hair was scrunched up and splayed across her pillow. She also had a dainty pool of drool by her mouth.

"Lila," Jessica whispered.

With a ladylike snort Lila shifted, but she didn't wake up.

"Lila!" Jessica hissed again, more urgently. She reached out and shook her friend's shoulder.

With a small gasp Lila awoke. Her big brown eyes shone like gold in the moonlight. "Jessica," she murmured sleepily, "what's the matter? What time is it?"

It was sometime after 1:30 A.M., but Lila didn't need to know that. "It's late," Jessica replied, taking a seat on the edge of Lila's soft feather bed. "I'm . . . I'm really sorry I woke you, but . . . I'm just way too messed up to sleep."

Lila sat up against the backboard of her bed and wiped her eyes. "Can this wait until morning?"

"No," Jessica replied, looking down at her hands in her lap. "No, it can't. I keep dreaming about Alyssa—"

Lila yawned. "Who's Alyssa?" she asked. "Oh, right, that girl you—"

"Right," Jessica said, her voice sharp with misery. "The girl I killed."

For a moment Lila sat in silence, staring at Jessica. A frown worked at Lila's mouth as she obviously sought the right words to say. *I have to give her credit,* Jessica thought. *I half expected her to immediately roll her eyes and say, "Whatever, Wakefield. Get over it."*

"You didn't kill her, Jess," Lila replied finally, shaking her head. "From everything you've told me, it sounds like you tried to *save* her."

"I did try," Jessica shot back. "And I failed. Which is the same thing as killing her."

Lila bit her lip. "No, it's not," she said. "It's completely different. You didn't throw her into the hole."

Jessica let out a short laugh and then wrapped herself up in her arms, suddenly shivering. Her own laugh had frightened her—it sounded so wounded and raw. "I killed her," Jessica repeated softly.

"OK. I have a story that might help," Lila said. She smoothed down the light, lacy blanket that covered her legs. "This one time my father was having a dinner party. You probably remember the night—the time we entertained for Bill Jozniak and his wife?"

"Oh, right," Jessica replied, confused. Bill Jozniak was a famous computer company owner. Mr. Fowler, who owned a silicon chip company, among other things, dealt with Mr. Jozniak on occasion. From pictures Jessica had seen in magazines and newspapers the guy was a major nerd . . . but incredibly, indescribably rich. And insanely powerful—he could have really hurt or helped Mr. Fowler's company. Lila had gone all out helping Mr. Fowler welcome the Jozniaks and other famous guests in style. But . . . "What does that party have to do with Alyssa?" Jessica asked.

"Well, that's the thing," Lila explained. "I don't think I told you this. I'm sure I didn't—it was way too embarrassing at the time. At that dinner party I helped Daddy do the seating arrangements, and you know what I did?"

"What?" Jessica asked, feeling drawn into Lila's story despite her sadness.

"I sat Greta Maylor next to Bill Jozniak!"

Jessica stared at her best friend, totally missing her point. Greta Maylor was an old movie star who had been famous for Jessica's whole life, but why was it a big deal for her to sit next to some rich computer nerd? "So?" she asked.

"Come on!" Lila protested. "Bill Jozniak owns megashares of the movie production studio that Greta Maylor was suing! I had totally forgotten. It was the *worst* faux pas. I nearly fainted."

"And you're telling me this because . . . ?"

Lila heaved a huge sigh. "I don't know," she admitted in a small voice. "At first I was thinking of telling you all this because I had ruined Daddy's big event and afterward he gave me credit for at least trying to help."

Jessica's mouth dropped open. "You thought that would make me feel better about *Alyssa?*" she asked.

"It doesn't quite work, does it?" Lila whispered, looking away. "It's not the same thing at all."

"No," Jessica said. "It isn't. Alyssa died. That's not a dinner party."

Lila was silent a moment, and then she directly met Jessica's gaze. "I'm sorry," she said. "I'm *really* sorry. About the whole thing with Alyssa. It's terrible. But I don't know what to say, Jess. I just know it wasn't your fault and—"

Jessica cut off Lila's words with a big hug.

"What was that for?" Lila asked when Jessica finally pulled away again. "Don't get all weepy on me, Wakefield."

"I won't," Jessica said. "It was just for . . . just for trying, that's all."

Elizabeth couldn't move. Her muscles wouldn't obey her. Something was holding her down, pinning her to the ground.

Eels.

Electric eels slithered up her face, over her chin, over her mouth. They were choking her.

Elizabeth screamed.

"Lizzie!"

Her chest heaving as she struggled to catch her breath, Elizabeth opened her eyes to see Jessica turning on the light. Jessica sat beside her on the edge of the bed and peered down worriedly. Elizabeth blinked. "I'm OK," she said, panting. "I'm OK."

"I know I'm not supposed to wake you," Jessica said, "but . . ."

Elizabeth moved over to give her twin more room. "No problem," she replied. "That nightmare

10

I was having—" Elizabeth shuddered. "I'm glad you woke me."

"Mine have been awful too," Jessica said. "I totally couldn't sleep." She frowned. "Are you sure it's OK that I got you up? The doctors did say you needed to chill for a while. The electric shock and everything."

Elizabeth was definitely tired but decided she actually felt all right—despite the terrible things that had happened to her.

That is, the terrible things that everyone had *told* her about.

Elizabeth herself couldn't remember a single event that had happened between the time the earthquake struck and hours later, when she'd finally regained consciousness. That chunk of time was completely blank.

"I'm fine," she told Jessica. "At least physically. I think I'm having these nightmares because my memory's gone—like my subconscious mind is trying to help me piece it together. I wish I could remember!"

Jessica sighed and slumped down onto Elizabeth's shoulder. "And I wish I could forget," she said softly. "What was your nightmare about? Did anything come back to you?"

For a second Elizabeth could only remember shifting, vague images, but then a picture of intertwining electric eels popped into her mind. She nearly gasped, struck with an unreasonable pang of fear.

"Uh . . . oh, I can't really remember," she answered, keeping her voice tightly under control. Elizabeth shook her head, trying to clear it. The last thing she wanted to do was dwell on frightening images she didn't completely understand, especially when her twin so obviously needed to talk about what was bothering *her*. "So . . . you had a nightmare too?" she asked. "About Alyssa?"

"Of course," Jessica said. She rubbed her eyes with her palms. "Every time I shut my eyes, it's like she's there, waiting for me, just staring and staring. I see her falling and hear her screaming, and then she tells me that I killed her." Jessica swallowed and then sniffled. "She's right, you know. I did kill her."

Elizabeth glanced at her sister. Jessica was staring straight out at nothing, her face a blank mask of shock. "You didn't kill her, Jess," she said, gently but firmly. "Alyssa's death was a terrible accident, but it was just that—an *accident*. I'm sure you tried your best to save her. But from what you've told me, there was nothing anyone could have done—"

"Oh, please," Jessica broke in. "Lizzie, you just can't know what it was like. When Alyssa was down that hole, totally panicking, I *promised* her I'd save her. I promised her!"

"And I'm sure you meant it," Elizabeth said. "Of course you did! You didn't know she'd fall before you could—"

"I failed, Liz," Jessica said flatly. "I failed, and now a girl is dead. I killed her. Can I say it any more plainly? *I killed someone.* Now can you really tell me I didn't?"

Elizabeth hesitated. "No," she told her twin. "I mean . . . *no,* you didn't kill her." But Elizabeth's protest sounded weak even to her own ears. There was nothing she could really say that could prove to Jessica that Alyssa's death truly was an accident—Jessica would have to learn that on her own, in time. "Hey," she said, pulling her legs out from under the light blanket that was covering her. "Do you have any idea how this happened?"

She pulled away a bandage from one ankle. Beneath the gauze were several angry-looking blisters near patches of tender, red skin. They looked like minor burns, but Elizabeth had no clue how she'd gotten them. And her knees were really scraped up—another total mystery.

Jessica stared at Elizabeth's injuries for a second, then closed her eyes and slumped down on the bed. "I have no clue," she said sleepily, snuggling in beside her twin.

Elizabeth ran her finger over the raw scrape on one knee. "Was I dragged anyplace while I was unconscious?" she asked. "Through the fire in our backyard?"

"I didn't get home until after you were rescued," Jessica mumbled into the pillow. "So I didn't see what happened to you."

"Mom and Dad were there, right? And Enid, of course. But who else was around who might know?"

13

Jessica didn't reply for a second, and Elizabeth assumed she'd fallen asleep. But then, her voice thick and weary, Jessica said, "I wasn't paying attention. I'd just killed Alyssa."

Elizabeth put her hand on her twin's shoulder and closed her eyes, stung by the pain in Jessica's words. *I guess I wouldn't have been paying attention to bystanders either if I'd just been through what Jessica experienced,* Elizabeth thought.

As Jessica began breathing more regularly, drifting off into sleep, Elizabeth racked her brain for any little scrap of memory of the earthquake's aftermath. Her dream about the eels was easily explained. Elizabeth had been told that someone had pulled her and Enid away from downed power lines. Those power lines certainly could be represented by electric eels in a dream. But she couldn't even picture the power lines in her head.

Elizabeth scrunched her eyes together, digging deeper into her mind. All she could recall, really, was the first moment the earth trembled . . . but then nothing after that until the fuzzy memory of waking up beside a groggy Enid. Elizabeth's mother's worried face was the first thing she'd seen, and then her father had helped her sit up. Jessica had run over, crying, to hug Elizabeth, and when Jessica had let go momentarily, Elizabeth had looked across the yard at the wrecked house. She'd seen an emergency medical technician leading Ken Matthews out of the house. Behind them two other EMTs had carried out Olivia's body. . . .

Olivia.

A whirlpool of sadness churned in Elizabeth's stomach. She wrapped herself in her own arms, pressing her lips together tightly. Olivia really was dead.

Elizabeth could barely believe it. She didn't *want* to believe it. Olivia had been one of Elizabeth's best friends for as long as she could remember—pretty much all through high school. They'd worked together on the student newspaper, the *Oracle,* and had eaten lunch together nearly every day. It seemed absolutely impossible that a funky, free-spirited girl like Olivia could be dead.

And she just got together with Ken Matthews, Elizabeth remembered. The tragedy seemed doubly poignant because Olivia had been so happy.

Elizabeth sniffled—there would always be a gaping hole in her life that Olivia had once filled with such zest and joy. *If I'm this sad,* Elizabeth thought, *what must Ken be going through right now?*

She couldn't even imagine. Apparently Ken had nearly killed himself trying to save Olivia, even threatening the EMTs with violence if they didn't help his trapped girlfriend. But Olivia had been crushed by the crumbled ceiling, and Ken's valiant efforts proved fruitless. Olivia was already bleeding internally by the time Ken ran off to get help, and he'd returned to find her dead.

Heaving a huge sigh, Elizabeth reached over

15

her sleeping twin and shut off the light. Ken had failed to save Olivia. Jessica couldn't save Alyssa. So many rescue attempts had gone so terribly wrong.

Except mine, Elizabeth realized. *Somebody rescued me and Enid. But who?*

Who had been near her when the earthquake hit? Who had been close enough to pull her away from the power lines?

There was only one person it possibly could be.

Devon Whitelaw—the brilliant, sexy guy who had thrown her love life into such upheaval in the past few months. The guy who had almost made Elizabeth forget the existence of her longtime boyfriend, Todd Wilkins.

Devon definitely had been right next to her when the earthquake hit—Elizabeth could remember that easily. He'd just given her a present . . . a book. That present came quickly to mind because . . . well, because it hadn't been what Elizabeth had hoped it would be. It had no romantic sentiments attached to it whatsoever, and that had certainly been disappointing.

But if Devon had rescued her . . . *wow.* How romantic.

There was only one problem. If Devon was the one who rescued Elizabeth and Enid, why hadn't he stuck around until they regained consciousness? Why did he vanish?

Maybe he just had to get home to check on Nan, Elizabeth thought. Nan Johnstone was Devon's guardian. *That makes sense.*

Sure, it made sense, but it still didn't explain how she'd gotten the minor injuries on her knees and ankles. Something about those scrapes and burns nagged at her memory. . . .

Devon will probably know, Elizabeth thought. *I'll go ask him as soon as I get the chance.*

Jessica moaned, turning in her sleep. It was a truly pitiful sound, and Elizabeth swallowed deeply, overwhelmed with sadness.

Jessica has good reason to be miserable, Elizabeth realized. *As do we all.*

Elizabeth closed her eyes and snuggled down next to her twin, hoping that she'd fall into dreams of happier times.

Chapter 2

Ken Matthews turned over in bed again, onto his stomach, trying to find a comfortable position. But his mattress and pillow seemed as hard and unyielding as they had in the last position he'd tried. Ken had been tossing and turning all night. His heart ached so badly, he could feel his pulse throbbing in his temples.

Ken stayed on his stomach for a few minutes, keeping his breathing regular and even. A memory swirled up from the darkness behind his eyelids. . . .

He was sitting at the corner table in Izzy's Incredible Ice Cream in the nearby town of El Carro, waiting for Freeverse, his Internet blind date. This was before he knew that Freeverse was Olivia's screen name, before he knew that Olivia was his soul mate. At the time he'd wondered what Olivia was doing in El Carro, but it hadn't even crossed his mind that Olivia could be Freeverse.

Out of nervousness and boredom, Ken had watched Olivia drink a soda and play with her wild, tangled mass of dark hair as she'd scribbled in her sketchbook to pass the time. Even though Ken had thought he was waiting for another girl, he'd been struck by Olivia's earthy, natural beauty.

The memory shifted. Olivia's hair was no longer wild, free, and shining. Now it was powdered with plaster dust, matted as it framed her bone white face. A thin line of blood streamed from her mouth.

Ken heaved the refrigerator that was pinning her down, preventing him from saving the life of the girl he loved. She screamed as the giant appliance rocked. Ken had to save her. He had to get her free! But he couldn't do it by himself. He just wasn't strong enough.

So he'd run out to try to find help, leaving her trapped.

Leaving her to die alone.

Ken sat up in bed. With a shaking hand he reached out and turned on the light near his bed. He'd never felt more miserable in his entire life.

When his eyes adjusted to the sudden bright light, the first thing they got a good look at was the portrait Olivia had painted of him just the other day. Ken crawled down to the end of his bed to get a better view.

The portrait had been a full-length nude study

of him in its first version, which Olivia had painted from her imagination, never having seen him totally naked. But the original had been pretty accurate, if he did say so himself—and incredibly embarrassing, especially when she announced she was going to display it at the school art show. Ken and Olivia had gotten into the biggest fight they'd ever had over that painting, and he'd thought he would never speak to her again. But Olivia had compromised, repainting the portrait to show only his head and shoulders.

Ken stared at the portrait, a tear trickling down his cheek. How he wished now that they'd never had that fight! If he'd known how short a time they'd have, he would have made sure that their every moment together had been truly, wondrously happy. What a waste to have spent his incredibly precious time with Olivia fighting.

Or was it? Ken wondered. *Maybe it wasn't a waste. If we'd never had that fight, I never would have found out how understanding she could really be. After that fight I only loved her more.*

He let himself slide off the end of the bed, landing on the floor in front of the picture. As he stared at the painting Ken felt as though he could sense her love for him in every brush stroke on the canvas. As if Olivia had been tracing her brush lovingly over the planes of his face as she'd painted. She had so much talent for art, but her real gift was how much she could love.

Ken shut his eyes, feeling dizzy with misery. *And now she's dead,* he thought bitterly. *I'll never again get to share that love. There will be no more wonderful paintings, amazing conversations, passionate kisses. . . .*

He opened his eyes again, staring at the painting. It seemed to mock the happiness he'd once had.

Ken had killed Olivia.

He never should have left her to die alone in the Wakefield kitchen. He should have thought of some way to save her. He should have been stronger, faster, smarter. He should have loved her more.

But he'd failed her. And now she was dead.

I don't deserve to enjoy her talent ever again, Ken told himself as hot tears cascaded down his face. *What's the point, when it only reminds me that I've lost the only thing that ever truly mattered?*

Ken angrily wiped away his tears.

He turned the painting around so that it faced the wall.

Devon Whitelaw revved his motorcycle as he sped up around a sharp curve. It was dark out on the cracked streets of Sweet Valley—especially since most of the street lamps were down from the earthquake—and going so fast was incredibly dangerous, even stupid. But Devon's thoughts and feelings were in utter turmoil, and he felt the need for some serious speed.

So what if I crash? he thought. *Maybe dying in a wreck of hot twisted metal is exactly what I deserve.*

It was nearly dawn, and Devon had been out riding his Harley-Davidson Sportster all night. Ever since he'd made sure that his guardian, Nan, was OK, he'd been buzzing through the wreckage of the town, loathing himself.

And for good reason, he thought as he headed out of Sweet Valley, up a road that led into the foothills on the coast. *I betrayed Elizabeth—a girl I thought I loved—when she needed me most. I should hate myself. Just like everyone else will hate me when the truth comes out.*

Devon ran a hand through his thick hair, shaking his head. He urged his bike to go faster up the winding road.

Why did I run from her? he asked himself. *I could have saved her easily. Why did I abandon the girl I knew was my soul mate from day one?* Devon had no good answers to those questions, so he zoomed recklessly up the mountain road, narrowly avoiding the rocky debris in his path.

Without even thinking about where he'd been headed, Devon had somehow arrived at Miller's Point, a rocky cliff that had an incredible view overlooking Sweet Valley to the east and the Pacific Ocean to the west. Devon had been told that generations of SVH students had driven up to the popular spot with significant others to be "alone."

Not anymore, Devon thought. He dismounted from his motorcycle and walked over to the edge of the cliff—which took two steps. The edge wasn't as far from the parking area as it had been. In fact, there wasn't any room to park anything larger than Devon's bike. Most of Miller's Point had crumbled down the hillside in the earthquake. Nobody would be driving their cars up here to make out ever again.

Devon sighed as he stared out over Sweet Valley. Pastel fingers of dawn were stretching up over the horizon, and by that early light Devon could see crumbled buildings, ripped-up roads, and fallen trees throughout the town. Small fires still burned on the perimeter, and a heavy haze of smoke lingered. Even from his high perch Devon could hear the faint wail of ambulance and fire-truck sirens. Sweet Valley was a disaster.

It seemed fitting that Miller's Point, the place where he'd shared such romantic, passionate times with Elizabeth, had crumbled down into ruins. If he still loved her, why had he left her to die in her backyard? Sure, he'd been terrified during the earthquake . . . that much he could admit to himself. It had been his first big quake since moving to California. He had a right to be frightened.

Even with those plausible rationalizations echoing

in his mind, Devon was still reeling with guilt. What kind of person abandoned the girl he loved to die—a coward, a betrayer . . . a monster? Or . . .

A survivor?

Devon quickly turned away from the view of the devastation of Sweet Valley to climb back onto his bike.

He'd run out of the Wakefield backyard, protecting himself at the expense of Elizabeth. Maybe that would seem horrible to anyone else, but Devon had learned at an early age that he had to take care of himself no matter what the odds. He'd survived his cold, distant parents . . . and their death. He'd survived his search for a new guardian, his move from the East Coast to California. He'd survived inheriting millions of dollars while surrounded by people who only wanted to feed off him in their greed. And now he'd survived a major earthquake.

Devon revved his engine again as he cruised down the rocky mountain road. *I did what I had to do,* he thought grimly. *Maybe no one else would ever understand. Maybe Elizabeth will hate me for it . . . but my survival always comes first.*

Always.

"Wasn't that Chez Sam?" Lila asked.

Jessica stared out the passenger side window of Lila's lime green Triumph convertible as they drove past a flattened, smoldering husk of a building.

Sure enough, Jessica could just barely make out the elegant script lettering on the posh French restaurant's blackened sign. "Oh, wow," she muttered. "It's gone."

"I'm positive they were insured," Lila said. "I happen to know that restaurants are required to buy all types of insurance . . . including earthquake."

Jessica slumped down in her seat, wishing she were anywhere else. "That's not the point, Li," she told her best friend. "Do you know how many dates I've gone to in that restaurant? Dozens. I remember I went there with that Pierre Du Lac guy—although his real name turned out to be just Peter Lake. But then I was calling myself Daniella Fromage at the time—"

"Fromage?" Lila asked. "Peter Lake? Isn't that the dude Dana Larson dated for a while?"

"After me," Jessica replied. "Remember when I got bored with all the guys at SVH so I joined that dating service? But I didn't feel like using my real name. . . ." She let her voice trail off.

"Yes?" Lila prompted.

Jessica shook her head sadly. "It doesn't matter," she said. "It's a long story." Jessica simply didn't feel like recounting a tale of her past wacky hijinks—especially when the restaurant that had been part of the story was now only a smoking ruin.

Both girls fell silent as they joined the long line

of slow-moving cars on the streets of downtown Sweet Valley. Lila honked her horn—a ladylike little toot. "Can you believe how many people are out to check out the damage? Vultures!"

Jessica didn't reply, unable to work up the energy to point out that Lila had dragged Jessica out of Fowler Crest that morning for the same purpose. Jessica hadn't wanted to come, but Mrs. Wakefield had insisted she get some fresh air. So now she was stuck in rubberneck traffic, surrounded by the most depressing sight she had ever seen in her life: a ravaged Sweet Valley.

As Lila guided the car through the streets, Jessica slipped into a funk. On the left was Hunt's Photography, where Jessica and Elizabeth had gotten their picture taken as a surprise Christmas present for their parents. The store was broken in two, cracked right down the middle like an egg. And up on the right was Jackson's Foreign Cars, where Jessica used to flirt with the hottie mechanics while the old Fiat Spider the twins used to share was being repaired. Now there was a giant cottonwood tree lying on top of the bashed-in garage.

"This is so horrible," Jessica whispered.

Lila nodded in reply, keeping her eyes fixed on the busy road ahead of her.

Jessica felt absolutely bleak inside, and the view around her just seemed to make *sense* somehow. *Like when Sweet Valley was beautiful and perfect,*

I felt beautiful and perfect too, she thought. *But now that I've killed Alyssa . . .*

Now that Jessica had killed Alyssa, her whole world had crumbled . . . literally.

Lila guided her Triumph off Main Street, turning down Ocean Avenue onto a block where all Lila and Jessica's favorite expensive stores were. On the left, the Silver Door, one of the most exclusive salons in town, seemed mostly intact, but nearby, the boutique where Elizabeth and Jessica had gotten their prom dresses—Mata Hari's—hadn't been so lucky. Its white stuccoed walls had crumbled.

As Lila and Jessica headed farther down Ocean Avenue, they came into the more residential part of town, which had suffered as much damage as the downtown area if not more. Lila eased her convertible around an overturned Range Rover that was partially blocking the road and then drove past a crew of workmen cutting up a fallen tree with a buzz saw.

"Isn't that Robin Wilson's old house?" Lila asked, pointing out the window to her right.

Jessica peered over. Sure enough, the house where Robin, Jessica's former cheerleading cocaptain, had lived had collapsed in on itself like a badly baked cake. "Good thing she moved away," Jessica said. "Seeing that would have broken her heart."

Nervously Jessica noticed that they were on the road leading to Sweet Valley High. She didn't know what she would do if SVH had been destroyed. The school had been such a central part of her life for so long, and if it had been hurt in the earthquake . . .

"Did you hear anything about the school?" Jessica asked Lila, unable to take the suspense any longer.

"Our school?" Lila asked. "I heard on the radio this morning that El Carro High was totally ripped apart."

Jessica clenched her teeth. "Who cares about El Carro?" she bit out. "Did you hear anything about *SVH*?"

"Sorr-*ree*," Lila drawled. "No, I didn't hear a thing."

Jessica braced herself as they approached . . . and then sighed in relief as the school—completely untouched—came into view. A few of the big white-oak trees flanking the building had fallen over, but the school itself seemed unscathed.

"See?" Lila said. "It's fine, Jess. Chill."

Jessica nodded, swallowing down her emotions. The survival of Sweet Valley High was something to be grateful for, however small. At least she wouldn't have to go someplace new and unfamiliar for her senior year.

But just as Jessica was feeling a little more relaxed, Lila gasped as she turned onto Parker Lane.

"What?" Jessica demanded.

Lila pointed ahead. Jessica squinted to see up

the road through the windshield. Her stomach sank.

The Dairi Burger.

Or what was left of it.

"Pull over!" Jessica insisted.

"I was *going* to," Lila replied as she steered the Triumph into the popular hangout's parking lot.

As soon as Lila cut the engine Jessica jumped out to survey the damage. The Dairi Burger looked awful. The planks of natural wood that had covered the exterior of the little restaurant had fallen down, split, or burned in a small fire that seemed to have consumed the entire place. The brown plastic sign on the roof with the words *Dairi Burger* spelled out in yellow script letters had cracked in three different places—which didn't really make a difference since the roof itself had partially collapsed. The front entrance had caved in, with the doors lying on the ground in pieces. Worst of all, an angry-looking jagged crack in the ground zigzagged under the foundation, causing the whole building to slump alarmingly to the left.

"I think the Dairi Burger is deceased," Lila said softly.

Jessica nodded. "It doesn't look very fixable, does it?"

"No way."

With a heavy sigh Jessica sat back on the rounded hood of Lila's car. "This is just terrible," she whispered. "The Dairi Burger. *Wasted.* It's like . . . it's like all those memories we had in that place . . . it's like they were just *erased.*"

"No," Lila replied. "Not even. I learned this when my house burned down, Jess. Memories stay with the person, with *you*, not with the thing that's gone."

Jessica was silent for a moment. "That was pretty deep, Li."

"Thanks."

"So what do *you* remember about the old DB?"

Lila took a deep breath. "Well, the first thing that pops into my head is . . . do you remember when John Pfeifer . . ."

Jessica didn't blame Lila for not being able to finish her sentence. John Pfeifer had tried to rape Lila, and that had messed her up badly for months afterward. He'd also partially burned Fowler Crest in retaliation for Lila exposing him as a rapist . . . although ultimately John had died in one of his own arson attempts. "I remember," Jessica said.

Narrowing her eyes at the shell of the Dairi Burger, Lila said, "I first confronted him in there." There was steel in her voice. "I went up to him and called him a rapist in front of everybody. That was the scariest thing I've ever done in my life."

"I remember the first time I saw Heather here," Jessica said. Heather Mallone was Jessica's latest cocaptain of the cheerleading squad and was nasty to the core. Sure, Jessica had to admit that

Heather was an excellent cheerleader, but that didn't mean she had to *like* her. From the first time Heather had shown up at the Dairi Burger, she'd been nothing but trouble. Jessica was glad Heather was graduating this year.

"Eww, Heather," Lila said. "Let's not think about her. I'd rather remember all the parties and victory celebrations after football games and all the fun stuff. All the time we spent here with Amy, Jeanie, and Sandy, gossiping about boys. That's prime time, Wakefield. We can't forget that!" Amy Sutton, Jean West, and Sandra Bacon were some of Lila and Jessica's best friends and, not coincidentally, sometime members of Jessica's cheerleading squad.

"All the double dates with Liz and Todd . . . ," Jessica brought up. "Like when I was dating Sam . . ." She shook her head. She still felt bittersweet emotions when she thought of Sam Woodruff, who she'd dated for several months. Sam had been killed in a tragic car accident, but what Jessica remembered most about him was how sweet he'd been and how much she'd loved him. The times she'd shared with him in the Dairi Burger had been some of the happiest moments in her life.

"Yeah," Lila said. "And just recently we had that party after the Battle of the Junior Classes. That was an absolute *blast*. You brought those cute Palisades guys with you—"

Jessica burst into tears.

Lila grabbed her shoulder. "What, Jess? We were talking about good times."

Jessica gasped for air through her tears. "Olivia . . . *Olivia Davidson* was there with us, with Ken," she sobbed. "And she's *dead* now. That was before . . . before I killed Alyssa. It all seems like a lifetime ago."

"I know what you mean," Lila said softly. "Maybe we should just go home."

With tears streaming down her face Jessica nodded, and Lila led her back to the car.

Jessica's heart felt just like the Dairi Burger— like the part of her that once loved fun and excitement now lay in rubble, destroyed.

With Alyssa's death weighing her down, Jessica knew that she wouldn't be able to enjoy anything ever again.

Chapter 3

Elizabeth felt relieved as she stepped through the big French doors of Fowler Crest and made a bee-line toward Enid Rollins's waiting car. She quickly climbed in the passenger side. "Hurry," Elizabeth told her best friend. "The sooner we're out of here, the better I'll feel."

Enid chuckled. "Not loving the posh life?" she asked. "Isn't it all champagne wishes and caviar dreams?"

"Hardly," Elizabeth replied as she secured her seat belt. "I feel like I'm suffocating in there. It sort of reminds me of the time Jessica and I went to Château d'Amour Inconnu." The twins had spent a few months as au pairs, taking care of the children of a royal family. It had been an amazing adventure but had only proved to Elizabeth that she wasn't the type to hang out with the rich and famous. "Mr. Fowler wears a *tie* to dinner every night. Can you even imagine living that formally?"

"Not really," Enid replied. She steered her car down the long, winding driveway that led out of Fowler Crest's sumptuous estate. "But it's awfully nice of the Fowlers to let you live there while your house is being repaired, right?"

Elizabeth smiled at Enid. "Of course it was wonderful of the Fowlers to open their home to us. I should be totally grateful, absolutely. And I am. But that doesn't mean I don't find their house chilly in an utterly snobby way. I just feel nervous around servants and feather beds and million-dollar Ming vases, that's all."

"I can understand that," Enid replied. "Jessica must be loving it, though. It's her dream to live like the Fowlers, isn't it?"

"Any other time I'd say you're right," Elizabeth answered, closing her eyes for a moment. "But right now Jess is way too messed up to enjoy anything. I'm really worried about her."

"She's taking that little girl's death really hard, huh?"

"Can you blame her?" Elizabeth asked softly. "I don't know if I could handle that myself."

Enid took one of her hands off the steering wheel and gave Elizabeth's arm a quick squeeze. "But I'm sure with the support of you and your parents, Jessica will pull through."

"I hope so," Elizabeth replied. "I've never seen

her worse off than she is right now. She's so sad, I don't . . . I don't even like to think about how bad she feels. It just *hurts* to think about, you know? That's why I'm so glad we're doing this today— going to town to see how we can help. I know helping other people is the only thing that will make me feel better."

"It was a good idea," Enid said. "But brace yourself. When I drove through downtown on my way up here, I saw . . . well, it's pretty bad out there. I know we'll find a lot of people who want to help, but the destruction is just overwhelming."

"I'll bet," Elizabeth whispered. "But I'm ready, I think. Where should we start?"

"Let's just drive into the town center and see what we can find to do."

Elizabeth nodded as Enid drove the car out of the posh hill section of town, where wealthy families like the Fowlers and the Patmans had made their homes, and into the more normal suburban area. Most of the expensive homes had been untouched by the natural disaster since they were built on more stable bedrock, so Elizabeth simply wasn't prepared for the destruction that greeted her. She gasped as she took in the flattened homes, upturned trees, and ripped-open roads all around them.

"I . . . I *thought* I was ready," Elizabeth stammered. "But . . . but this . . ."

"I know," Enid said. "It's awful, isn't it? And wait . . . it gets worse. Downtown was the hardest hit."

The girls fell silent as Enid drove downtown. Elizabeth felt deeply shocked and unable to find words to express how shaken she was by the toppled homes. All her life Sweet Valley had seemed like a safe haven, a quaint little town that was a refuge from all the difficulties life had to offer. It had been the most perfect place on earth. But if such misery could ravage Sweet Valley, no place would ever feel safe again.

On the outskirts of the downtown area Elizabeth sat up straight. They were passing by The Fast Lane, a bowling alley where Elizabeth had occasionally gone with friends. It was completely smashed, with the giant neon bowling pin that used to be on its roof now in shards in the parking lot. Never again would Elizabeth laugh as she rolled another bowling ball into the gutter. At the corner Enid took a turn down a more residential street.

"Oh, isn't that Ronnie Edwards's house?" Elizabeth asked. The entire row of houses on this block had been gutted by a fire.

Enid nodded somberly. "Yeah," she said. "I still can't believe he's dead, Liz. I know Ronnie didn't treat me all that well when we dated, but still . . ."

Elizabeth bit her lip. "The news must've hit you pretty hard."

"It did," Enid admitted. "Do you remember finding him?"

"Me? Finding him?"

38

"You must have blocked that out too," Enid said. "Caroline said you found Ronnie's body. . . ."

Elizabeth's mind flashed back on black leaves, a lifeless arm. Her stomach flopped—and then the memory was gone.

"I don't remember anything," she said, dazed.

"It's probably better that you don't," Enid said grimly. "Oh, look, Liz! Patty Gilbert's house is trashed too!"

"Poor Patty! Where are all these people going to go?" Elizabeth asked. "It will be ages before these houses can be rebuilt! Is everyone just going to move away and start again someplace else?"

"I really don't know," Enid replied. "The whole community will have to come together to save this town. I don't even want to think about all the work that needs to be done."

The Plaza Theater suddenly came into view. Elizabeth felt a sharp pang of sadness as she saw that the theater's marquee had fallen down. She'd gone to the old classic-movie house quite often with Enid and Maria Slater . . . and even more often on dates with Todd.

Todd.

Elizabeth closed her eyes and shook her head. She definitely didn't want to think about Todd Wilkins. The simple thought of her longtime boyfriend—her *ex*-boyfriend—and his warm, coffee-colored eyes hurt her deeply. Elizabeth had experienced so much difficulty with Todd in the recent past. She had no idea if she'd ever be able to be friends with him again, never mind date him. She had to think about something else—fast.

"Will Maria be joining us in town?" Elizabeth asked Enid quickly.

"Maria Slater or Maria Santelli?"

"Slater." Elizabeth counted both Marias among her closest friends, but she hung out with Maria Slater, a former child actress with flawless ebony skin and a fierce, down-to-earth sense of humor, much more often.

"No," Enid replied. "The Slaters left town for a few days to stay with Maria's aunt until their house can be fixed."

"Was the damage bad?" Elizabeth asked.

Enid concentrated on steering around a group of tree limbs that had fallen into the road before she answered. "Not terribly," she said. "I think their basement flooded, that's all. Maria said she'd definitely be back in time for Olivia's funeral, if not sooner."

Elizabeth glanced at her best friend, trying to keep from bursting into sudden tears. "I keep forgetting," she murmured. "Olivia . . . it doesn't seem real, does it? It doesn't seem . . . *possible* somehow that she's . . ."

Enid shook her head and quickly wiped away a tear that was rolling down her cheek. "I can't believe it. I . . . I don't know what we're going to do without her."

"I know," Elizabeth said morosely.

Life is so fragile, Elizabeth thought. *If Ken is feeling even a fraction of the sadness I'm feeling . . . I can't even imagine how he's handling it. Especially after trying so hard to rescue Olivia.*

Elizabeth tapped Enid gently on the shoulder. "Hey," she said. "Do you have any idea who rescued *us?*"

Enid glanced at Elizabeth, surprise obvious on her face. "I . . . I just assumed it was Devon," Enid replied. "Wasn't it? I mean, I already told a reporter who called that Devon saved us."

"I thought so," Elizabeth said. "I assumed the same thing. But why do *you* think it was Devon? And why did a reporter call you?"

"I woke up for a few moments while you were still unconscious and I heard you muttering his name," Enid said. "I figured you were calling out to him to thank him. And the reporter was just calling homes in town, looking for human-interest stories for the news. I'll bet they don't even use my story, though—not with all that's happened in Sweet Valley. Anyway, who else could it have been except Devon?"

"I can't think of anyone," Elizabeth replied. Her heart lurched a little as she imagined Devon dragging her bravely to safety, risking his own life. . . . It proved how much he really loved her! "The second we get a chance, we have to thank him," she said.

"Absolutely," Enid agreed. "But how do you thank someone for saving your life? Nothing seems quite adequate, you know?"

"We'll think of something," Elizabeth said. She blushed a little as her mind conjured up the perfect way to thank Devon . . . with an incredibly passionate kiss.

"We were really lucky, Liz," Enid said, interrupting Elizabeth's warm thoughts.

"You can say that again," Elizabeth replied.

Enid pointed up the road at a girl standing near the partially crumbled supermarket. "Look! Isn't that Maria Santelli?"

Elizabeth nodded. "Pull over," she suggested. "Let's see what she's doing."

Maria waved as Enid pulled up beside her. The pretty, brown-haired girl was a cheerleader on Jessica's squad, but she was actually better friends with Elizabeth. Maria seriously dated one of Elizabeth's closest friends, Winston Egbert, the class clown, and was the most community-minded girl Elizabeth knew. Which only made sense since her father, Peter Santelli, was the mayor of Sweet Valley.

"Hi," Elizabeth called to Maria as she climbed out of Enid's car. Maria quickly stepped over and grabbed Elizabeth in a big hug.

"I'm so glad you're OK," Maria told Elizabeth sincerely. She disengaged and hugged Enid too. "Both of you. It's so awful about Olivia."

Elizabeth nodded. Enid, Maria Slater, Winston, Maria Santelli, and Olivia had all eaten lunch with Elizabeth during nearly every school day of their junior year. The death of Olivia left a gaping hole in their close-knit circle of friends that could never be repaired.

"I miss her already," Enid said solemnly. "I feel so bad for her family . . . and Ken, of course."

"Truly horrible," Maria agreed. She took a deep breath. "I made my father give me something to do to take my mind off everything. So right now I'm looking for volunteers to help set up a refugee center down the street. My father's getting the Red Cross to give us supplies. Do you guys want to help?"

"Just tell us what to do," Elizabeth replied. "We're all yours."

"Great," Maria said. She smiled warmly but sadly. "I knew I could count on you."

"Oh, look, The Foxy Mama has been completely wrecked!" Lila joked to Jessica as she drove through the streets of Sweet Valley on her way home, pointing at a small, crushed, clothing boutique. "Their clothes have been out of style for so long, I wonder if anyone will notice."

Jessica didn't reply.

Lila bit her lip and stole a glance at her best friend. No laugh, no smile, *nothing*. Lila had never seen Jessica so bummed out.

Sure, she saw Alyssa die right in front of her, Lila thought. *Which is majorly horrible, no doubt. But why is Jessica acting like it's all her fault? It was an accident!*

The whole situation was completely confusing.

Still, Jessica was her best friend. If Jessica was hurting, Lila had to try to help. *I have to remember my promise to myself,* Lila recalled. During the earthquake she'd been trapped in the Wakefield bathroom with Todd Wilkins. While she and Todd had been panicking together, Todd had accused Lila of being shallow, of not really caring about anyone besides herself. She'd sworn to herself that she would try to be more open and honest with the people she really cared about. Life was too short to waste it being snobby.

But remembering her promise didn't help her come up with any good words of wisdom that would make Jessica feel better. Lila had no idea what to say.

Jessica, you have to get over this, she practiced telling her friend in her mind. *Moping around won't bring that girl back to life, now, will it?*

Lila shook her head. That just seemed harsh and not at all caring and supportive. Irritated with herself, Lila honked her horn at some old man in a station wagon who was driving much too slowly in front of her. To Lila's relief, the station wagon took the next left, clearing the road.

Jessica, get real, Lila tried again. *Life is short and nasty. That girl could have been hit by a bus while you weren't even around!*

With a wince Lila realized she was on the wrong track. Pointing out to Jessica that life could be horrible wasn't the way to cheer her up!

With a big sigh Lila gave up. She simply hadn't had enough practice being kind and warm to make a difference in Jessica's black mood. She wasn't Elizabeth Wakefield, giving out advice at every opportunity.

"Hey, Jess, check it out," Lila said, gesturing with her head in the direction of a collapsed bank on the right side of the road. "The poor little Union Bank. I'm so glad my father closed his account there. Their service was always just dreadful!"

Again Jessica didn't acknowledge that Lila had even spoken. And Lila couldn't help wondering if her words seemed as shallow and flighty to Jessica as they sounded to her own ears. *Not that it matters,* Lila thought as she slowed her Triumph behind a few other cars at a red light. *Jessica's not paying any attention to me anyway.*

As the light turned green Lila noticed a group of men and women helping to clear the rubble away from the entrance to the Shop and Hop, a twenty-four-hour convenience store. Lila thought she recognized one of the guys lifting a fallen beam of wood.

It was Todd.

Lila's heart gave a little, unexpected leap. She quickly pulled into the Shop and Hop's parking lot and cut her engine.

"I'll just be a sec, OK, Jess?" Lila asked as she opened her door. Jessica seemed too lost in misery to care, slumped over against her window, staring straight out at nothing. Lila shrugged and headed over to Todd.

She had no idea what she was going to say to him, but she was oddly pleased to see him. Todd heaved the beam he was carrying into a pile and then turned around to see what else he could clear away. He was dressed in a T-shirt and jeans, with his dark brown hair falling into his face. His big basketball-player muscles glistened with sweat. He looked sexy. *In a grimy, slumming, working-class kind of way,* Lila amended. *But then . . . I have to remember that Todd's not working class! He's rich!*

Before she could stop herself, a memory of the moment before she and Todd were rescued in the Wakefield bathroom popped into her mind. They'd been comforting each other, terrified that they were going to die in the fire licking at the bathroom window. Todd had leaned down, his face only inches from hers, and she'd been certain that he was going to kiss her. . . .

Lila's heart thudded in her chest at the memory. The EMTs had burst in before their lips had touched, and now Lila couldn't help wondering what that kiss would have felt like.

"Todd," Lila called out. "Hi!"

Todd looked up. "Oh, hey, Lila," he said flatly.

She immediately felt disappointed. Lila wasn't sure what she had expected, but a little more enthusiasm would have been nice.

"Can I talk to you for a moment?" she asked. "Privately?"

Todd seemed surprised. "Lila," he said. "We're in a parking lot. Where can we have privacy?"

Lila nodded toward the edge of the lot. "Over here," she replied. "It'll only take a second."

Todd sighed, but he followed Lila away from the other workers. Lila stopped in the corner of the lot, where she was sure they wouldn't be overheard.

"What's this about?" Todd asked. "Are you OK?"

"I'm fine," Lila assured him. Suddenly she felt incredibly nervous and unsure of what she wanted to say to him. "Um . . . I just wanted to tell you how much I appreciate . . . I wanted to thank you for . . . how helpful you were . . . when we were trapped." She had a sudden, almost irresistible urge to tell him how sorry she was that they hadn't gotten a chance to complete their kiss.

"That's cool," Todd said. "It could have been a lot worse."

"That's so true," Lila replied with a laugh, tossing her long brown hair.

"Well . . . ," Todd said. "I really have to go back and help now, if that's all you wanted to say. If we don't clear out the entrance to the Shop and Hop, there are a lot of people who won't be able to get any food, with the supermarket destroyed and everything."

47

That's it? Lila wondered, suddenly flashing with hot anger. *No "Lila, I can't stop thinking about you?" No "Lila, I've been dying to kiss you?" What's the* matter *with him? And to think I was about to tell him how much I wanted to kiss him!*

"Oh, there is one other thing," Lila said icily. "If you ever—and I mean *ever*—tell anyone what almost happened between us in that bathroom, I swear I will kill you!"

"What?" Todd asked, obviously taken aback.

"You heard me!"

"Fine," Todd spat out.

"Fine!" Lila replied. She turned around and stomped back toward her car.

He agreed so quickly! she thought as she pulled open the door to the Triumph and sat down next to Jessica in a huff. *He doesn't want anyone to know about us either!*

Lila clenched her teeth as she started up the car, her entire body filled with frustration.

The connection we made obviously meant nothing to him!

Todd stared after Lila as she zoomed her little sports car out of the Shop and Hop parking lot, feeling a heavy wave of disappointment settle over him—even though he knew he'd just done the right thing. It was obvious that Lila had wanted him to disagree with her angry statement about not telling anyone about their near kiss, but Todd couldn't lead her on. That wouldn't be fair . . . to her or to him.

"Hey, Wilkins!" a voice called. "We need some help over here!"

Todd turned around and strode back to where the other workers were struggling with a large piece of Sheetrock that had fallen off the roof. He quickly helped the others carry the chunk of rubble over to a pile they had made a few yards from the entrance.

Todd wiped his hands on his jeans. *How can I start anything with her when I'm not over Elizabeth yet—not by a long shot?* he wondered. *Plus I'm leaving for camp. . . .*

The idea of spending all summer in Sweet Valley without Elizabeth hadn't appealed to Todd, so before the school year had ended, before the earthquake, he'd signed up for a summer basketball camp in North Carolina. He was leaving in just a few days.

My life is crazy enough as it is without adding Lila Fowler to the mix, he thought.

Todd bent over and started collecting smaller pieces of fallen roofing tile. *There's just no room in my life for anyone as obviously high maintenance as Lila!*

But he couldn't stop the memory of their near kiss from replaying in his mind. She'd closed her eyes as he leaned down to her, and she'd quivered in his arms. . . .

Todd shook his head and added the pieces of tile he'd collected to the big pile of debris.

No, he thought. *No way! Yes, Lila's beautiful and fascinating . . . but . . .*

But the emotions Lila brought out in Todd were too much to handle.

And that was that.

Chapter 4

"C'mon, Jess," Elizabeth cajoled. "Come with me. Just for a few minutes."

Jessica crossed her arms over her chest and turned away.

Elizabeth stared out at the ocean waves and silently wished they still had the Jeep. Driving with the top down was always a pick-me-up. But the new Jeep was on a long waiting list at the shop after suffering minor damage in the earthquake. Still, Elizabeth had been sure that this trip to the beach would help cheer up her miserable sister, but so far Jessica had refused to get out of their mom's car.

Elizabeth had to try. Besides, she needed a walk on the sand at sunset herself. After she'd gotten back from helping set up the refugee center with Maria and Enid, she'd found herself alone at Fowler Crest, haunted by memories of Olivia. It seemed as though every time she was alone with her thoughts, the realization that she'd never see one of her best friends again tore her apart. Elizabeth had been desperate to get out of the house and do something.

Elizabeth had enlisted Mrs. Wakefield's help in forcing Jessica into the car. Mrs. Wakefield had only been too happy to help—the whole family was getting very worried about Jessica's lengthy stupor. So Jessica had come along, but Elizabeth knew that the view of the Ocean Bay Beach parking lot wasn't going to lift Jessica's spirits.

"Please, Jess," Elizabeth tried again. "You love the beach . . . and it's always so beautiful at this time of day."

"Can't you just leave me alone?" Jessica whined.

"No, I'm not going to leave you alone until you at least *try* to feel better," Elizabeth answered. She'd never been more worried about Jessica in her life—and that was saying something.

Jessica stared ahead in stony silence.

Elizabeth opened the car door. "OK!" she announced. "I'm going to take a walk. Are you sure you won't come?"

Jessica just glared at her.

"Jessica, it's the ocean," Elizabeth wheedled. "You know it always has such a good effect on your state of mind. You were practically born on this beach—"

"If I come with you," Jessica interrupted

sharply, "will you shut up and stop bothering me?"

"Sure!" Elizabeth agreed. Anything to get her sister out of the car.

"Fine," Jessica said, climbing out and slamming the door behind her.

At the edge of the lot Elizabeth removed her sandals and held them, dangling, from one hand. The cool, white sand felt wonderful under her feet as she stepped onto the beach. As Elizabeth crested a large dune, followed by her dawdling sister, she got her first good look at the ocean.

The water was still very choppy from the earthquake, and a lot of the beach's sand had been sucked out to sea in the huge waves that always followed tremors. There was a thick line of drying seaweed, shells, waterlogged tree limbs, and other flotsam far up the beach—much farther than the ocean waves were reaching now. Seabirds circled above the line of waste, swooping and pecking at unfortunate creatures that had been washed up on the sand as they called to each other with their high, piercing cries. Elizabeth crossed the line, stepping carefully through the dead jellyfish and sea grass, and headed directly for the water.

As the first wave lapped at her feet Elizabeth jumped back. The Pacific Ocean was painfully cold as usual. But Elizabeth was content to stand at the edge, staring out at the soothing display of crashing whitecaps on the tips of the water's waves. The sun was setting on the horizon, and the first streaks of pastel pink and orange were spreading across the sky as the bright red ball of fire seemed to melt into the ocean.

A cooling breeze scented with seawater ruffled Elizabeth's hair, and she exhaled a long breath, immediately feeling more relaxed. She spotted a toppled lifeguard's stand and moved to sit on a fallen gray plank. After a moment Jessica sat beside her.

The twins sat quietly for a while, staring out at the churning waves, letting the ocean work its soothing magic. Elizabeth could feel her worries easing away with every sheet of water that slid up the beach.

This . . . this is why we live in Sweet Valley, Elizabeth realized. Much of the man-made stuff might have fallen down, but the beach would always be beautiful. More than anything else, sitting at the edge of the water at sunset felt like home to her.

The ocean makes me feel so . . . so insignificant, Elizabeth thought. Next to the vastness of the body of water in front of her, her problems felt petty and small and, well, manageable. At least for a little while.

Elizabeth peeked quickly at her twin. A tear was rolling down Jessica's face, but her expression wasn't nearly as miserable as it had been. The ocean was having its healing effect on Jessica too, just as Elizabeth had hoped it would.

She reached over and gave her twin a hug. Jessica squeezed back tightly, as though afraid to let go.

After a long moment of holding her sister, Elizabeth finally sat up again. "So," she asked softly, "you want to take a walk?"

Jessica nodded. "OK," she said.

As they ambled along the shoreline, Elizabeth tried to put her finger on the exact reason why Jessica's stupor seemed so strange and upsetting. It wasn't that she'd never seen her sister sad before. After Jessica's boyfriend Christian Gorman had died in a gang fight, Jessica had been truly miserable, but even that didn't seem as bad as this bout of sorrow. During that tragedy Jessica had still seemed like Jessica—as though she would eventually return to her old self after some time had passed. But now . . .

Now that bright spark that makes her who she is just seems extinguished, Elizabeth thought worriedly. Worst of all was Jessica's new silence. For the first time in her life Elizabeth actually missed her twin's constant mindless chatter about boys, clothes, cheerleading, and going to all the best parties. The loss of that was a terrible thing to witness.

Maybe this walk will help her snap out of it, Elizabeth hoped. *I don't expect her to come back completely, but maybe, just maybe, the ocean will help her see that life is still worth living despite Alyssa's awful death.*

Up ahead on the beach Elizabeth could just make out the Beach Disco, a favorite spot of Jessica's. In fact, both twins had enjoyed some of the best parties of their lives there. Elizabeth had even been planning to throw Jessica a big surprise dance party at the Beach Disco for their seventeenth birthday, although plans had changed at the last minute.

As the girls hiked closer to the disco Elizabeth suddenly stopped short.

The Beach Disco was built off a rocky outcropping that jutted out onto the beach, with the dance floor suspended over the ocean on tall stilts. But the enormous waves had knocked the stilts out from under the dance floor. A full half of the Beach Disco had collapsed into the ocean, with broken planks of wood and pieces of the dance floor washing up on the shore. The Beach Disco had been ripped apart.

Terrified that Jessica would take the awful sight really hard, Elizabeth tried to make a joke. She turned to her twin and attempted a smile. Jessica was staring at the Beach Disco, her face an expressionless mask.

"Uh . . . ," Elizabeth began. "It's a good thing we didn't have your surprise party there!"

Jessica slowly turned to face her. For a long second she didn't say a word. But then she started to shake. "It's a *good* thing?" she asked incredulously. "You think that's a *good* thing?"

"Jess," Elizabeth said quickly, "I didn't mean—"

"Oh, no," Jessica broke in, her voice rising. "It's *better* that Olivia died in our house and that Ronnie was killed by one of our fallen trees! It's *better* that you were almost killed by power lines in our backyard!" Jessica's face turned bright red as her words rose to a scream. "No, no, no, Lizzie, you're right! It's so much *better* that I ran out of the house to get more ice and then stopped on the way home to help poor Bryan Hewitt *kill his little sister!* Can't you see how much *better* that was?"

"Jess, I'm sorry," Elizabeth protested, taking a step back. "I wasn't thinking—"

"Everything I've ever enjoyed is dead!" Jessica hollered. "Crushed like the Beach Disco. And you know what, Lizzie? You know what? I wish I was dead too!"

With those terrible words Jessica turned around and ran back up the beach toward the car, trailing miserable, angry sobs in her wake.

Elizabeth stood for a moment in shock, staring after her twin. Somehow she'd managed to say exactly the wrong thing. Feeling stunned and close to tears herself, Elizabeth finally hurried after her sister.

She's much worse off than I could have dreamed, Elizabeth thought. *And now I have no idea how to make things better again.*

If that's even possible anymore.

Mr. Wakefield pulled the family station wagon into their driveway and killed the engine.

"Here we are!" Mrs. Wakefield chirped. "Is everybody ready?"

"I am, Mom!" Elizabeth replied, just as cheerfully.

Jessica cringed. Her mother and sister's happiness was so totally fake. They were obviously trying to keep everyone's spirits up, but their faux glee was really, *really* irritating. Jessica had to press her lips together to keep from snapping out a nasty reply.

Instead she peered out the wagon's window, staring up at the charred remains of the house in which she'd grown up. A big section of the roof had caved in, and a full half of the structure had burned—it was completely unrecognizable as the cute little house it had once been. The southernmost corner had fallen off the rest of the house, revealing singed, broken furniture speckled with melted insulation.

"OK, gang," Mrs. Wakefield said as she opened her door. "Remember, don't go in the kitchen. The fire department said that area of the house is unsafe, but the rest is stable. And don't worry about the big furniture. We've decided that it's all pretty much a write-off. Just collect whatever small things you can find, especially things with sentimental value. Let's do it!"

"I'm going to go straight up to my room and start there," Elizabeth said. "Is that all right?"

Mrs. Wakefield smiled. "I think that's just fine," she replied.

How can anyone look at that mess of a house and still sound so perky? Jessica wondered, shaking her head. *Looking at it just makes me want to curl into a ball and stay like that forever.*

Mrs. Wakefield and Elizabeth got out of the car and headed toward the house, but Mr. Wakefield didn't move. His hands gripped the steering wheel, and he appeared to be holding his breath.

Jessica and Mr. Wakefield watched Mrs. Wakefield and Elizabeth approach the house up the walkway. Mrs. Wakefield unlocked the front door, which made absolutely no sense to Jessica—after all, there was a hole in the side of the house big enough to drive a truck through.

Mr. Wakefield cleared his throat, and Jessica leaned forward, resting her elbows on the top of the car seat in front of her. "Your mother and sister are such troopers," he said, glancing back at her. "I don't know where they're finding the strength."

"Major denial," Jessica replied. "Steven's so lucky he got to go back to school to check on his apartment."

Mr. Wakefield managed a small smile. "We do have to go in there. Are you ready?"

"Nope," Jessica answered.

"Me either," Mr. Wakefield said. "Let's get out of the car, though. We don't want them coming back to check on us, now do we?"

Jessica knew that another blast of her mother and sister's forced cheerfulness very well might finish her off. She opened her door and stood next to her father on the edge of their lawn.

Mr. Wakefield put his arm around his daughter and squeezed gently. "It's just a house," he said softly.

"Are you telling me or yourself?" Jessica asked.

"Both of us," he replied. "It's something both of us need to remember. No matter how bad it looks, it's only a house, and houses can be rebuilt. We've already spoken to contractors about fixing it up again. It'll be nice to move into a brand-new house, won't it?"

"I guess," Jessica said with a shrug.

"Good." Mr. Wakefield hugged Jessica again and then looked directly into her face. "Now all you have to do is go up to your room and see what keepsakes you can salvage. I know you can handle that."

Jessica wasn't sure what she could or couldn't handle anymore, but what was she supposed to say, pinned there in her father's gaze? "OK," she replied. "I'll try."

"That's my little girl," Mr. Wakefield said.

Jessica followed her father across the lawn and into the house. The small chandelier that hung above the foyer had fallen and smashed on the floor, but the living room beyond wasn't as bad as Jessica had feared. True enough, the furniture was ruined—the fire hadn't reached the living room, but the smoke had blackened the couch and the walls, and the television had toppled off its stand. There was also an angry-looking crack that crossed the ceiling, but generally, looking at the damage didn't make Jessica feel as sick as she'd thought it would. It *would* be cool to get a whole new set of living-room furniture.

Mr. Wakefield joined his wife at the bookshelves, and Jessica turned to check out the staircase. It seemed to be in pretty good shape, so she carefully made her way upstairs. When she reached the hallway, Jessica took a deep breath and entered her bedroom.

It was totally trashed.

The flames hadn't spared any of Jessica's stuff. Her purple walls were blistered and cracked, and her bed was a charred slab. Most of the clothes that usually littered the floor were in ashes, along with lumps of melted CDs and tapes. The curtains on her blown-out windows hung in tatters, and her posters of rock stars Jamie Peters and Ryder Mitchell were in cinders, curled up and unrecognizable. For a long moment Jessica just stared at the wasteland that used to be her bedroom, her mouth hanging open in shock.

But then she took a long, deep breath to fortify herself and began picking through the rubble for anything that might have survived.

From under her bed Jessica pulled out a surfboard. It was yellow and turquoise, and the sight of it caused Jessica's heart to lurch. She was extremely relieved to see that it was still in pretty good shape. It had been protected by the bed, and only a few scorch marks marred its surface. Jessica hugged it, lost in warm memories of Christian Gorman, to whom the surfboard had belonged. Christian had taught Jessica to surf, his tan, muscular arms holding her afloat as she paddled on the unfamiliar board for the first time. And she'd used the board to win the Rock TV surfing competition—

a victory dedicated to Christian's memory.

Oh, Christian, Jessica thought sadly as she used the surfboard to start a "to-keep" pile near the door, *I wish you were here now. I wish you could take me away to live in a big sand castle in the sky, like you promised when you were alive.*

Pushing away her bittersweet thoughts of Christian, Jessica returned to sifting through the mess in front of her. The end table beside her bed was made of heavy oak and seemed mostly intact. In its little cabinet Jessica found the dirt bike helmet that had belonged to Sam Woodruff. Jessica held the helmet in her arms, sniffling as tears threatened to overwhelm her.

Jessica had never dated a guy for longer than she dated Sam. He'd been her equal in so many ways, and they had been absolutely inseparable. She'd never met a guy who could keep up with her energy and enjoyment for life the way Sam could. He'd been so sweet, but so exciting. Jessica could easily recall the thrill she always got watching him race his dirt bike. Sam had even come to her rescue when she'd stupidly joined up with that horrible Good Friends cult! But he too had died in a terrible accident after the midyear Jungle Prom.

After placing the helmet down beside Christian's surfboard, Jessica stood staring at the mementos.

How could I have been so foolish as to ever think life was fun? she wondered miserably. *What kind of shallow monster have I been? All the time I was surrounded by death and never realized it.*

Trying to ignore the heavy weight of sadness pressing down on her, Jessica wandered over to her dresser to see if any of her jewelry was still OK. She poked through the warped and misshapen chains and earrings in her jewelry box, but nothing looked good enough to keep. Then Jessica noticed a small gold puddle on one end of the dresser. She stared at the puddle for a moment, trying to figure out what it had been before the heat of the fire had melted it down. Suddenly it struck her—it was her PBA pin.

Phi Beta Alpha was the most exclusive sorority at SVH. Jessica had done everything she could to get herself and Elizabeth into it, and although Elizabeth eventually resigned, claiming the group was too snobby, Jessica had been elected president. Jessica could easily recall how much she had coveted that pin before she'd become a member of the PBA and how pleased she'd been to wear it when she'd finally passed all the hazing rituals. A memory of the time she'd dyed the school cafeteria's mashed potatoes purple as part of her pledge tasks almost made her smile, but when her gaze fell on the little gold puddle again, she had to turn away to keep from bursting into tears.

I've got to find something happy in here, she thought as she scanned her bedroom desperately. *There must be something!*

Jessica spotted the corner of a red-and-white item of clothing sticking out from under a pile of burned-up schoolbooks. *Yes!* she thought as she quickly kicked away the books. *My cheerleading uniform!*

As cocaptain of the cheerleading squad, Jessica had cheered Sweet Valley High's sports teams to victory time and time again. There was nothing she enjoyed more than performing amazing acrobatic stunts in front of the crowded school bleachers, knowing that the attention of everyone was focused directly on her. If anything could cheer her up, holding her uniform in her hands would certainly do the trick.

As soon as the books were removed, though, Jessica gasped. Her pom-poms had melted over the uniform, ruining it. It was worthless.

Jessica sank to the sooty floor. *All my memories are worthless,* she thought. *It's like they belong to a different Jessica, a Jessica who isn't me anymore. That Jessica thought life was fun and exciting, filled with adventure. But she was seriously deluded.*

Hot tears trickled down Jessica's face. *I have no idea who I am anymore,* she realized. *I've got no PBA pin, no cheerleading uniform . . . All the things that made me who I am have been destroyed.*

And life isn't all fun and parties and cute guys like I always stupidly thought. Instead it's tears and sorrow . . . and death.

With those terrible thoughts echoing in her mind, Jessica rolled onto her side on the burned carpet and wept.

Elizabeth's room had never been so messy in her life. Usually she kept it as neat as humanly possible, with a place for everything and everything in its place. *Oh, well,* she thought with a sigh. *I guess there's not much I can do about* this *mess—after all, the room's been through an earthquake and a fire!*

Most of her books had been destroyed—even her favorite one, the copy of Christina Rossetti's collected poems that she'd read and reread. Her big stack of back issues of the school newspaper, the *Oracle,* featuring all her old "Eyes and Ears" columns as well as the newer ones that included her "Personal Profiles" column, was now just a pile of cinders. And her laptop computer and all her disks were too badly damaged to be saved.

Most of the photographs she'd tacked up on her bulletin board above her desk had crinkled and blistered, but a sweet one of her and Todd at the beach seemed mostly intact. *Except for Todd's head,* Elizabeth amended as she peered at it more closely. The corner of the shot had been burned away, taking Todd's head with it. Her eyes filled with tears as a wave of sadness crashed over her. But she couldn't get distracted by sorrow now. She had to stay focused.

Elizabeth turned to her bureau and began filling a bag with the clothing inside. From her T-shirt drawer she pulled out a funky, brilliantly colored shirt that DeeDee Gordon had made. DeeDee was a talented artist and often sold her T-shirt designs at a store called Blue Parrot Crafts, although Elizabeth had been given this one as a gift. She smiled as she stuffed it into the bag. Her clothes smelled smoky, but that would probably come out in a wash.

After she had collected all her clothing and placed it in her to-keep pile, Elizabeth looked around the room to see where else she should check.

Oh, I almost forgot! she thought. *The top of my closet— there are a lot of keepsakes up there!*

Standing on tiptoe, Elizabeth reached up to the shelf, and her hand closed around a stack of bound notebooks. *Thank goodness,* she thought as she pulled the books down. *My diaries are fine. I don't know what I would have done without these!*

After placing the diaries in her to-keep pile, Elizabeth went back to the closet and pulled down a trophy—her second-place award from the national cheerleading competition. With a smile Elizabeth remembered how long and hard Jessica had campaigned for Elizabeth to join the squad for the competition. Eventually Elizabeth had struck a deal with Jessica, and to her surprise, cheerleading had been really fun! *Well,* she amended, *at least it was fun after all the bitter squabbling between Jessica and Heather finally settled down.* Cheerleading wasn't something that Elizabeth wanted to spend a lot of time doing, but the trophy went into the to-keep pile too.

Assured that her closet was empty, Elizabeth circled her bed, searching for anything else worth keeping. Beside her desk she noticed a strangely shaped plastic lump. *What is that? An old stuffed animal?* she guessed as she knelt to peer at it. There was a zipper on the side, so that couldn't be right. *A gym bag?*

Then she figured it out. It was her school backpack, burned almost beyond recognition. Elizabeth chuckled. She'd carried that backpack with her for nearly the whole school year, and now it looked as unfamiliar as something that had fallen from outer space!

Amazingly, the zipper still worked. Inside was a mostly empty notebook, which was as ruined as the bag around it. Behind that was a textbook, which Elizabeth pulled out. She had to open it up to find out what the subject was since the cover was completely blackened.

Chemistry.

Elizabeth sat back on her heels, suddenly lost in memories of Devon. He'd been her lab partner in Mr. Russo's chemistry class for the last few months of junior year. It was during chemistry class that she had first fallen in love with Devon. He was something of a genius at science, and he'd used his exceptional knowledge to perform little experiments designed to flatter her. Elizabeth felt a warm tingle as she remembered him mixing acids and bases together in a test tube until he had matched the green-blue color of her eyes.

I've waited too long to thank him for rescuing me, Elizabeth thought as she closed the textbook and put it aside. *I'll stop by his house later this afternoon.*

Chapter 5

"Can you even believe this?" Amy Sutton gushed to Lila as the girls wandered through the warped and cracked halls of the Valley Mall. "It's a dream come true!"

"My dreams usually aren't this crowded," Lila replied irritably as she was once again forced to step aside to allow a swarm of people past her. "And what do I care if they're having a sale? I can already afford anything in here I want."

Amy sniffed. "Well, some of us aren't so lucky," she said, pulling her long blond hair over one shoulder. "To us lowly peons, this earthquake sale is the shopping event of the year, Li. Imagine, twenty percent off *everything* in the entire mall! It's . . . almost unbearable. I don't even know where to start."

How about in Brains "R" Us? Lila thought

uncharitably. *You could sure use an upgraded model!* She'd been cranky since she woke up. Between worrying about Jessica and thinking about Todd, Lila had barely gotten any sleep. And Amy, who could be a mindless Chatty Cathy at the best of times, had been way wired all morning. Besides, Lila did not like crowds—and the sale had brought people out in droves, especially since the damage to most of the stores in the mall had been minor.

"Lila?" Amy prompted. "Did you hear me? I said I didn't even know where to start. No suggestions from the shopping queen?"

"Lisette's, I suppose," Lila responded with a sigh. "I heard Nadine has a new line in." Nadine designed all the best clothes that Lisette's Boutique had to offer. "And we might as well try Bibi's too." At least the exclusive clothing stores Lila had mentioned wouldn't be as crowded as the hallways of the mall—the salesclerks in both shops were intensely fierce if they didn't think a customer could afford their wares.

"Don't forget Kiki's!" Amy chirped. "That's my fave!"

Of course it is, Lila thought. *Which explains why you always dress like a refugee from some third world nation.* But she just nodded at Amy's suggestion. Why not? Lila had nothing better to do today—besides sit at home and wonder why Todd hadn't shown up at her front door, begging to see her. Yet.

Amy pointed out a woman shopping on crutches, her leg wrapped in a fresh white cast. "Look at that," she said. "That woman was probably injured in the earthquake, but already she's out shopping. So many people are such desperate shopaholics, they just *need* to shop . . . like, to forget their empty lives—"

"Amy—," Lila tried to interrupt.

"It's so sad," Amy continued as though Lila hadn't even spoken. "If that woman would only realize that her inner child is crying out for attention, she wouldn't need to hobble around on crutches, trying to fill the void in her life with shopping."

Lila groaned. For a while now Amy had been very active with a group called Project Youth, where she answered phone calls on a hot line for troubled teenagers. Sure, it was great that Amy helped out kids with problems, but Lila very much wished that all the trendy psychology that Amy had picked up at the hot line hadn't infested her conversation so thoroughly. Amy constantly spoke in "psychobabble," as Jessica had termed it.

Today Lila was in absolutely no mood to deal with Amy's clueless comments. "That is *not* why everyone's out shopping," she snapped. "To feed their inner children. Please. People's stuff got destroyed in the earthquake, and there's a sale. Duh."

Amy stopped short, causing people behind her to grumble as they were forced to avoid her. "It was just a thought," Amy said in a hurt voice. "You

71

don't have to completely invalidate me."

Lila was about to show Amy exactly what invalidation *really* felt like, but then she remembered again the promise to herself to try to be less shallow and snobby, to be more open and real with people. And that meant dealing with Amy's feelings. "I'm sorry," she told her friend. Those two words felt very strange to say. Lila had not apologized to Amy since they'd first met in middle school.

For a moment Amy's face was a complete mask of shock, but then she broke out in a big smile. "That's cool," she said cheerfully. "Think nothing of it."

"I won't," Lila replied, smiling back. "Now let's get to shopping before this crowd buys out the entire mall."

The girls had traveled only a little way toward Lisette's when Amy grabbed Lila's arm. "Hey, check it out," Amy said. "There's Bruce over in Casey's, stuffing his face with a banana split."

Lila peered over at Casey's Ice Cream Parlor, where handsome, rich Bruce Patman was indeed eating a large sundae, sitting at a table beside a large broken plate-glass window, which seemed to be the only damage Casey's had suffered. "So?" Lila asked.

"So . . . should we go talk to him? I haven't seen him since the twins' party, and I still haven't gotten used to the idea that he won't be around next year."

"I don't see why not," Lila replied. "But just for a few seconds. That's about all the Bruce I can take without screaming."

Lila and Amy breezed into Casey's. "Hello, Patman," Lila said coolly.

Bruce glanced up. "Well, well," he said, showing all his white, even teeth in a totally fake grin. "If it isn't two of the prettiest new seniors at Sweet Valley High. I hope you'll enjoy *high school,* girls, while I'm off in the real world at college. Try not to miss me too much."

"In your dreams," Lila said pleasantly.

Bruce laughed and gestured for the girls to join him at his table.

Amy sat down across from Bruce, and Lila slid into the next chair, glancing in irritation at her watch.

"So, Bruce," Amy began, leaning across the table toward him, "are you all packed up for SVU already?"

"Not even," Bruce replied. "There's still a month to go before I leave. Hey, did I tell you that I was accepted into the business program? It's easily the most prestigious department at SVU, bar none."

Lila smirked. "And the new wing of the SVU library your father donated had nothing to do with that?"

Bruce's mouth dropped open in shock. "How'd you know—," he sputtered. Then he regained control of himself and glowered at Lila. "Oh, right," he said. "Your father's on the board of directors at SVU, isn't he?"

"And I have all the inside info," Lila replied. She stood up. "Well, Ame, we'd better motor." Lila had already had as much as she could stand of Bruce in one dose without breaking into hives. "Patman," she said, "it's been real."

"*Fowler,*" Bruce replied, mimicking her haughty intonation, "I'd say keep in touch, but we both know that's not going to happen, don't we? I'll be sure to spare a thought for you while I'm hooking up with all the hottest babes on campus."

"Whatever," Lila said. She turned to leave.

"Bye, Bruce," Amy said as she followed Lila out of Casey's.

"Lila, wait up!" Amy hollered down the hallway, and Lila slowed to let her friend catch up. "You know . . . ," Amy panted once she had reached Lila's side, "I had a thought back there while you were bantering with Bruce."

"And what was that?" Lila asked.

"The fact that anyone would have to be *blind* not to notice the sparks flying between you two," Amy replied with a big smile. "It might have been a mistake never to have made a Patman-Fowler romantic merger, hmm?"

Lila gasped, deeply shocked and offended. "Get *real*, Amy," she said. "The very thought makes me want to puke."

"I don't know," Amy teased. "I think you'll miss ol' Brucie more than you're letting on."

Lila wheeled around and glared at her friend.

"Amy Sutton," she said sternly, "I can swear to you right now, I will never, *ever* date Bruce Patman! Not as long as I live! The very thought is . . . absolutely *absurd.*"

Amy just smiled.

Feeling incredibly miffed, Lila stalked down the hall. Amy was out of her mind, obviously. *Bruce Patman, indeed,* she thought with a sniff. *As though I'd even consider that nightmare remotely dateable!*

Although, Lila realized, *if Amy knew who I really can't stop thinking about, the whole world wouldn't hear the end of it. If she even had an inkling that I've been obsessing over kissing Todd Wilkins—*

Lila stopped in her tracks, her stomach dropping. Amy bumped into her from behind, but Lila didn't react to Amy's squawk of surprise. Directly ahead of her, as though thinking about him had conjured him up from thin air, was Todd himself, heading toward Sam's Sporting Goods.

Suddenly Lila didn't care what Amy thought. She walked briskly over to Todd, determined to head him off before he disappeared into the store.

When she got close enough, Lila tapped him on the shoulder. Todd jumped a little, surprised. As he turned to face her, Lila's first thought was: *He's such a babe!*

Lila simply couldn't forget how wonderful it had felt when Todd had recognized the real, frightened core inside her during the time they'd been trapped together. Something about Todd Wilkins made Lila want to be a better person, someone he would respect, someone he would want to protect.

"Hello," she said, hoping that this time he'd look glad to see her.

But as Lila met his warm brown eyes Todd quickly glanced away.

"Uh . . . oh, hey, Lila," he replied nervously. "It's good . . . it's good to see you."

"How sweet of you to say so," Lila said. Then she put on her best haughty, dispassionate expression—one she knew was laced with pure ice. "Even if it is a total lie."

Yes, Lila had sworn that she'd try to be more open and less snobby. But she'd go to her *grave* before she made herself vulnerable to an insensitive jerk like Todd Wilkins.

Todd winced as he repeated Lila's words in his mind.

Even if it is a total lie.

Man, she was some piece of work! *But can I blame her for being rude to me?* Todd asked himself as he stared down at his shoes. *It must be really obvious that I'm not all that psyched to see her.* In fact, Lila was the last person on earth he'd wanted to run into at the mall.

Todd had been replaying his memory of their near kiss all day. Even when he'd *wanted* to think about something else, the memory had stubbornly lingered, and that had left him feeling cranky, confused, and out of sorts. He definitely wasn't in the mood to take Lila's rudeness lying down. And her nasty comment was the last straw.

He glanced up. Lila rolled her eyes at him and turned to leave.

"I'm surprised you can even recognize a lie when you hear one!" he called after her. "Shallow people usually can't, you know."

Todd gulped as Lila slowly turned to face him. Her eyes were blazing.

"*What* did you say to me?" she asked.

Amy Sutton suddenly appeared beside Lila. "Lila's not shallow!" Amy said shrilly. "And what would you know about it anyway, you big dumb jock?"

As if dealing with Lila wasn't complicated enough, now Todd had to deal with Amy's two cents too? He decided to ignore her. "You heard me," he told Lila.

"So I'm shallow, am I?" Lila said calmly, taking a deliberate step toward him. "Maybe I am. But I can recognize a lie when I hear it, and I can recognize a liar when I see one."

"Yeah?" Todd said. "Well, you—"

"And believe me, Todd," Lila interrupted in a loud, imperious voice, "I'm not lying when I say that you don't know me well enough to say if I'm shallow or not. Whatever you say, you don't know me!"

"Isn't that what you're all about?" Todd

snapped back. "Making judgments about people before you know them because of how rich they are or how they look? Isn't that what snobs like you do?"

"She does not!" Amy piped up. "Lila has never—"

Lila sharply held up her hand in front of Amy's face, and Amy fell quiet. "I'll deal with this," she said, without ever taking her eyes off Todd.

She was truly angry now, and he definitely would be lying if he said that the fire in her eyes didn't scare him more than a little. She approached him until she was close enough that Todd could have . . . well, he could have kissed her if he hadn't been afraid that Lila would bite him first.

"And what about when people get to know *you*?" Lila purred. "What about someone who dated you for an entire year? What did Elizabeth Wakefield see in you that made her jump all over Devon Whitelaw? Can you answer that?"

"Ooh," Amy said.

For a long moment Todd couldn't speak—he was too shocked and hurt by Lila's words to even think coherently. He felt as though Lila had just poked a stick into the hornet's nest of his worst insecurities and stirred.

But he couldn't let Lila think she'd won. "You don't . . . ," he began through gritted teeth, "you don't even have the right to say Elizabeth's name!" Todd's hands began to shake as anger surged through him. "You don't even know what you're

78

talking about! If you had one-tenth the decency and kindness Elizabeth has . . ."

Todd let his voice trail away, his anger suddenly deflating. *Why am I arguing for Elizabeth's decency and kindness?* he wondered, feeling bewildered. It wasn't as though Lila had invented what had happened between himself and Elizabeth. In fact, Elizabeth had hurt him worse than any other human being ever had before. Elizabeth had left him for Devon—that was undeniable, if incredibly painful.

He glanced at Lila and was completely surprised to see that his comparison of her to Elizabeth had hit home. Her bottom lip was trembling, and her eyes were welling with tears. But as soon as she saw that Todd was looking at her, Lila's face immediately became a placid mask again. Without another word, Lila pivoted gracefully and strode away.

Amy shot Todd a look filled with daggers before following her friend down the busy corridor of the mall.

Todd pressed his hand to his forehead as he watched them until they disappeared into the crowd. He was suddenly struck with the urge to run after Lila, apologize profusely for comparing her to Elizabeth, and then grab her and kiss her as he'd been wanting to for the last few days.

Todd closed his eyes and shook his head until the urge passed. *Am I crazy?* he wondered. *Is*

*there something about me that just enjoys pain?
Lila has got to be one of the nastiest people I've
ever known!*

But it would be some kiss, that he knew for
sure. He'd be a total fool not to see that. It was so
obvious that all the lightning that crackled around
her when she was fighting would easily translate to
the electricity of a kiss.

Todd turned back toward Sam's Sporting Goods
and stepped inside, forcing himself to think about
the errand that had brought him to the mall in the
first place. He needed a new duffel bag for basketball camp.

Think about the boring duffel bag, he ordered
himself. *And nothing else.*

Todd couldn't wait to leave Sweet Valley and set
out for North Carolina. He was counting the minutes until he could get out on the road, leaving his
mess of a life behind.

Chapter 6

As the doorbell rang, Devon laid his hammer aside with a groan. He'd been trying to repair a window frame in the downstairs guest bedroom that had cracked during the earthquake. But Nan wasn't home, so he'd have to answer the door himself.

This had better be important, Devon thought as he stomped toward the front door. *I am not in the mood to be polite.*

Devon yanked open the door and found himself face-to-face with Elizabeth. Right behind her was Enid Rollins.

They know, was Devon's first thought as his mind reeled with panic. This was the moment he'd been fearing—the moment when Elizabeth accused him of abandoning her after the earthquake. *What will I say?* he wondered desperately. *She's going to hate me forever!*

"Hi," Elizabeth said. There was a strange, whirling intensity in her eyes that he couldn't identify. Whatever she was thinking, it surely couldn't be anything good.

"How's it going?" Devon replied, blood pounding in his temples. "Uh . . . I'm kind of busy right now."

"That's OK," Elizabeth said. "This will only take a second. I just want to ask you a question."

"Not now," he said, beginning to close the door. "I can't right now. Uh . . . I'll catch you later, all right?"

But before he could close the door completely, Enid stepped inside. And to Devon's utmost surprise, she grabbed him around the waist in a big hug.

"Um . . . uh . . . ," Devon stuttered, staring down at Enid's head. "What's that for?"

Enid released him and stepped back, looking up at his face with a big smile. "So modest," she said. "As if he didn't know!"

"Huh?" Devon replied.

"I know nothing I can say is really enough," Enid continued, "but I—" She gestured toward Elizabeth. "That is, *we* . . . well, we couldn't let another day go by without saying thank you. For saving our lives."

"You must be joking," Devon said, deeply confused. "I don't think this is very funny."

Enid laughed. She glanced back at Elizabeth, who smiled too.

Is this some horrible nightmare? Devon wondered. *Are they just trying to torture me?*

Elizabeth took a step into the house. "It was you, wasn't it?" she asked. "It had to be. Nobody else could've been there to drag us out of danger."

Devon stared at Elizabeth, his mouth gaping open. For a long moment he stood in shocked silence, feeling absolutely bewildered. *What is she talking about?* he asked himself. *Dragged them out of danger . . . ?*

But then he figured it out.

Oh, wow, he thought. *They think I saved them!*

The whole idea was so completely wrong that Devon was temporarily left without his power of speech.

"C'mon, Devon, confess," Enid said. "We know it was you who saved us. Don't bother with the false modesty."

He couldn't let this go on any longer. Devon had to tell them the truth . . . didn't he? He opened his mouth to tell Enid that she had the wrong guy, but then he caught a good look at Elizabeth's face.

She was smiling brightly and looked even more beautiful than the angelic image of her that haunted his dreams. In her lovely blue-green eyes there was nothing but pure admiration.

And it was all for him—for the guy she believed had saved her.

Devon's heart melted. He loved Elizabeth. He had no idea why they thought he had saved them, but there was no way he could look at the depth of happiness in Elizabeth's eyes and crush it with the truth.

Knowing he would regret it but unable to stop himself, Devon stepped forward and wrapped Enid in a hug. "I was glad to," he said.

Over Enid's shoulder Devon stole a peek at Elizabeth. She was standing in his doorway, beaming at him. For a moment his heart leaped. Elizabeth loved him! The girl he loved returned his feelings. Nothing felt better than that. Nothing.

Devon disentangled himself from Enid and turned toward Elizabeth. She threw her arms around his neck. As he pulled her close, inhaling her clean, wonderful scent, he realized that he'd never before felt such warmth of love for a girl as he did in Elizabeth's embrace.

But then Devon shuddered.

Because Elizabeth's love was based on a lie.

Elizabeth sighed happily in Devon's arms. She held on as he trembled slightly against her, his strong muscles bunching. *He feels it too,* Elizabeth thought. *He can feel how much we're meant to be together.* She was hugging her hero, and that made it amazingly more exciting.

Finally, reluctantly, Elizabeth pulled away. "So . . . ," she said, gathering herself together again, "what happened? I mean, what did you do to save us?"

A look of surprise flickered across Devon's face.

"What do you mean?" he asked back. "Don't you know? You were there!"

Elizabeth blushed, embarrassed by her blank memory. "Actually," she explained, "I can't remember a thing. After the earthquake started . . . well, everything after that is just *gone*. I must've been shocked by those power lines pretty badly."

Devon turned to Enid. "And you don't remember either?"

Enid shook her head. "Nope," she replied. "I didn't wake up until you had already left."

"Oh," Devon said. "Let me see. Um . . ." He gestured with his hand toward Elizabeth. "You and I ran over to Enid after she was knocked out. She was out cold on the ground, and the power lines were all around her. We each grabbed one of her arms and started pulling her away from the danger area. But you were hit by one of the lines before we could get away. After that it gets a little hazy because I was pretty freaked out. But I think I kept pulling Enid until she was safe, and then I ran back in to get you."

"Incredible," Enid whispered. Then she turned and grabbed Elizabeth's hand. "You tried to save me too," she told her. "I guess I should also thank you."

Elizabeth smiled at her best friend. "It's kind of a waste, though, since I don't remember being that brave!" she said with a laugh. "Devon was obviously the real hero here."

"It was nothing," Devon said, sounding oddly

tired. "It's what anyone would have done."

"Anyone with a heart as big as yours," Elizabeth told him warmly. Even though she'd been wildly attracted to him before, now her feelings seemed to have multiplied. If Enid hadn't been standing right there, Elizabeth wouldn't have been able to stop herself from kissing him. She felt her face growing hot.

Suddenly Elizabeth was struck by a strange recollection: She was on her knees in her own backyard as the ground trembled. *Devon!* she had screamed at the top of her lungs. She was full of anguished dread as the all too familiar image of the electric eels slithered back into her mind.

Elizabeth blinked away the frightening thoughts. The images had seemed so real that she immediately knew they were a missing fragment of her memory. *But that's it?* she wondered, feeling annoyed. *It's not enough! It doesn't make any sense!*

How she wished she could remember everything that had happened! She felt so helpless, so out of control, as if her brain were willfully disobeying her.

I'll just have to assume that I was screaming at Devon in panic over seeing Enid unconscious and in danger . . . and that the eels are just a representation of the power lines, she thought.

It was funny, though, because the eels hadn't quite *seemed* like power lines in the burst of memory she had just experienced. They'd seemed more like snakes.

Something nagged at the corner of Elizabeth's

mind, something to do with a snake. . . .

Enid bumped Elizabeth on the shoulder. "Hello, Liz!" Enid said with a laugh. "Where did you just go?"

Elizabeth ducked her head. "Sorry. I didn't mean to drift off like that. But I think I just remembered something about the earthquake."

"What?" Devon asked quickly. "What did you remember? Uh . . . anything important?"

"Not really," Elizabeth admitted. "Nothing that makes any sense to me anyway!"

"OK, good," Devon said, sounding strangely relieved. "I mean, it's good that you're starting to remember."

"It is a good sign," Elizabeth agreed. "I can't wait to remember everything. Hey," she said, "you wouldn't happen to know how I got these burns on my ankles, would you? Or these scrapes on my knees? I keep thinking they're important, but I don't know why."

"Nope," Devon replied abruptly. "Sorry. And . . . well, I don't mean to be rude, but I promised Nan I'd repair a bunch of stuff in the house before she got home this afternoon. So if you guys don't mind . . ."

"Oh, sorry," Enid said. "You said you were busy." She gave Devon another quick hug. "Thanks again, really."

"Don't mention it," Devon said.

As Enid walked outside, Elizabeth stepped up for her turn to say good-bye.

"Thank you," she whispered. "For my life."

Devon shook his head and didn't reply, closing his eyes as he pulled her to him. Elizabeth rested her cheek against his muscular shoulder, squeezing him with her arms. He rocked gently as he held her and placed a kiss on top of her head.

"Do you think . . . ," Elizabeth began, looking up into his face. "Could we get together—do something together when things have settled down? Like a movie, I guess?"

Devon smiled. "I'd like that," he said.

"Great," Elizabeth replied, returning his smile. "I can't wait."

Later that night Jessica slipped under the covers of her bed in the Fowlers' guest room. *Off to sleep for another night filled with nightmares,* she thought as she closed her eyes. *Whoo-hoo.* Why couldn't she be happy in her dreams at least? But even that small comfort had been denied her since the earthquake.

A soft knock made Jessica open her eyes again. "Yes?" she called. "Come in."

Mrs. Wakefield opened the door and poked her head into the room.

"I just stopped in to say good night," Mrs. Wakefield said softly. She entered the room and sat on the edge of Jessica's bed.

Jessica immediately curled around her mother, feeling near tears as Mrs. Wakefield began stroking her hair.

"We're all terribly worried about you, sweetheart," Mrs. Wakefield said. "We really haven't had much of a chance to talk since the earthquake, and I'm sorry for that. But I'm here for you if you want to talk about that poor girl."

Jessica sat up and collapsed into her mother's arms, bursting into tears, her face buried in Mrs. Wakefield's shoulder. "It was all my fault, Mom," she sobbed. "I *killed* her. Alyssa's death was all my fault!"

"Shhh," Mrs. Wakefield whispered. "Shhh. It wasn't your fault, honey, really it wasn't. It wasn't anyone's fault. Alyssa's death was a tragedy—that's undeniable—and I wish more than anything that you could have been spared seeing it. But it was an *accident*. You were trying to *rescue* her. Can't you try to believe that?"

"No, I can't," Jessica replied miserably. "I know whose fault it was. Mine."

Mrs. Wakefield sighed. "I'd like to convince you otherwise," she said, "but I have a feeling that nothing I can say will do any good. But maybe *doing* something will help."

Jessica wiped her nose on the sleeve of her T-shirt. "Like what?" she asked.

"Elizabeth and her friends have set up that refugee center downtown," Mrs. Wakefield answered. "If you're feeling guilty—and I'm definitely not saying you should be—maybe working at the center will help you resolve your feelings."

Jessica let go of Mrs. Wakefield and rolled onto her back. "Won't it be hopelessly geeky there?" she asked. "With all Elizabeth's friends . . ."

"Jess!" Mrs. Wakefield scolded. "That's not very kind of you. Besides, Elizabeth has told me that Maria Santelli has set up the center. And she was a member of your cheerleading squad, wasn't she?"

"Yeah, but . . ."

"But what?"

"But I don't know if I can handle it," Jessica whined. "All those people's lives have been messed up. What good will I be? They won't even want me there."

"They need all the help they can get," Mrs. Wakefield countered. "I'm going to stop by and lend a hand myself. I think this is something you should do, Jessica. Will you give it a try?"

"I guess," Jessica agreed reluctantly.

"Good," Mrs. Wakefield said. "It will make you feel better, I promise."

Jessica nodded once and then grabbed her mother in a big hug. "I love you," she whispered.

"And I love you," Mrs. Wakefield replied. "With all my heart. Now try to get some sleep, Jessica. You've got a big day tomorrow at the refugee center."

Jessica smiled and turned onto her side, closing her eyes.

Mrs. Wakefield kissed Jessica on the forehead, ran her hand over her daughter's hair, and then left the room, shutting the door behind her.

With a long exhalation of breath, Jessica tried to look forward to tomorrow. Maybe hanging out with people from school and keeping herself busy would help her keep her mind off Alyssa.

And maybe, just maybe, she would start to feel like her old self again.

Chapter 7

"Thank you, Suzanne," Elizabeth said politely. She was standing behind a long folding table in the basement of the community center, surrounded by boxes of donations people had already dropped off. "All this food and clothing will help a lot of people."

Suzanne Hanlon nodded. "I'm glad I could help," she said. "I just wish it was more."

Elizabeth blinked, stunned that normally snobby Suzanne could be so kind and charitable. When Elizabeth had first seen her walk in with the boxes, she figured Suzanne was in it for the tax write-off. It seemed the earthquake had changed a lot of people.

After Suzanne had glided away, Elizabeth began to sort the new goods, taking advantage of a momentary lull. The refugee center had been a zoo all morning, and she was already feeling over-whelmed. Across the room Elizabeth could see Enid at a table with Maria Santelli and her mother, Cindy, giving out medical supplies. Near them Nora Dalton, the popular French teacher at SVH, was handing out boxes of food and jugs of water with the help of Winston Egbert and his father, Sam. Winston's mother, Sharon, was at a table with Mrs. Wakefield, distributing flashlights, candles, and batteries. On the other side of the big, crowded room, Elizabeth watched momentarily as Bert and Emily Wilkins found proper clothing for a family that had lost all their belongings.

Elizabeth quickly averted her gaze before Mr. and Mrs. Wilkins spotted her staring at them. She felt a little weird being in the same room as Todd's parents since she was barely speaking to him.

After filling a cardboard box with canned food, Elizabeth closed it and pushed it over to the side. She wondered where Jessica had gone. They'd arrived together with their mother, but Jessica had quickly disappeared. Biting her lip, Elizabeth allowed herself a moment of worry about her twin before she began filling the next box. Would Jessica ever be able to shake the misery that had engulfed her? And what would happen if she couldn't?

"Hey, Liz," Maria Santelli said, interrupting Elizabeth's thoughts. "It's kind of slowed down over here, huh?"

"Yeah," Elizabeth replied. "But it's amazing how much people have already brought in."

Maria nodded, looking tired. "We'll need a lot more if we're going to make a difference to the people who have lost everything," she said. "Actually, I came over here for a reason. I need someone to help with the temporary home placements. Would you be interested in doing that?"

"Sure," Elizabeth answered. "What would I have to do?"

"I'll explain on our way upstairs," Maria said, gesturing for Elizabeth to follow her. "All you have to do is match up homeless families with other families who have offered to open up their houses until repairs can be made."

"That doesn't sound so hard," Elizabeth said, following her friend up a short flight of stairs.

Maria gave a snort of amusement. "Oh, yeah?" she replied, opening the door to the lobby. "Check this out."

Elizabeth gasped. A long line of people stretched down the hall and continued all the way outside the doors of the community center. "All these people lost their homes?" she asked, horrified. "I . . . I had no idea it was so bad."

With a nod Maria opened the door to a small beige office at the far end of the hall and ushered Elizabeth inside. "Pretty awful, isn't it?" she said.

Elizabeth nodded. Of course, she had lost her home too, but the Wakefields had been lucky enough to be friends with the Fowlers and were very comfortable in their temporary home. What would all these people do? Finding placements for them seemed like an impossible task.

"But there's hope," Maria said. "Look at this." She handed Elizabeth a clipboard with a sheaf of paper on it. "This is the list of people who responded to my father's plea to open up extra rooms in their homes."

Elizabeth quickly scanned the list. She almost burst into tears of pride as she saw the pages and pages of donors. It seemed like nobody in Sweet Valley had refused Mayor Santelli's request. *It's so wonderful how this town sticks together,* Elizabeth thought, wiping her eyes.

"Pretty cool, huh?" Maria asked.

Elizabeth nodded, still struggling to regain control of her emotions. "It's . . . it's amazing," she finally managed to say. She sat down behind the desk and placed the clipboard in front of her. "But why am I in this office?"

"My mother suggested that the families might like a little privacy while they're being matched up," Maria explained. "I thought it was a good idea too. I could totally see people starting to squabble over who gets placed where. So privacy seemed like the best option."

"That makes sense," Elizabeth replied. "Well, then . . . why me? Why not some adult?"

Maria smiled. "Don't take offense to this, Liz,

but, well . . . you're *you*. OK? I'm going to leave you to it, and I'll send in the first person on my way out. Are you ready?"

"As I'll ever be," Elizabeth answered. "I'll see you later, Maria."

"And thanks, Liz," Maria said as she left the office. "I'll send a replacement in for you in a couple of hours, but tell me if you get exhausted. You're a lifesaver!"

Elizabeth tried to prepare herself as the first family entered the room, but she couldn't disguise her shock at seeing Roger Collins walk in along with his six-year-old son, Teddy. "Mr. Collins!" she blurted.

The tall, handsome teacher with strawberry blond hair and blue eyes was Elizabeth's favorite instructor at Sweet Valley High. She'd been in his English class, and he was the adviser for the *Oracle*, but more than that, Elizabeth considered him a trusted friend. He'd always been willing to listen to any problem Elizabeth had suffered over the past year and often had been extremely helpful to her—as well as to dozens of other students.

"Hello, Elizabeth," Mr. Collins said. He sat down in a chair across from her and pulled Teddy into his lap.

"What happened?" Elizabeth asked. "Is your house—"

"My house was buried in a landslide, and my sister, Heather, just moved to Florida. We have

97

nowhere else to go. I'm afraid I'm feeling rather desperate."

Elizabeth nodded sympathetically. "Don't worry," she assured Mr. Collins. He had always been helpful to her, and now Elizabeth was very pleased to be able to return the favor. "We'll find you someplace to live, I promise."

A few minutes later Elizabeth had matched up Mr. Collins with Irene and Bob Bacon, Sandy Bacon's parents, who had noted that they didn't mind small children staying with them. And Elizabeth knew from several occasions when she had baby-sat Teddy that he could be quite a handful.

"I don't know how to thank you, Elizabeth," Mr. Collins said as he got up to leave.

Elizabeth nodded, feeling close to tears. "Don't thank me," she replied. "Save your thanks for the Bacons. They're the ones who deserve it."

For the next few hours Elizabeth threw herself wholeheartedly into helping people—most of whom she'd known her entire life. Finally Enid entered the office just as Patty Gilbert and her parents were leaving. Elizabeth had set up the Gilberts with the Morrows.

Enid smiled. "How's it going?" she asked.

Elizabeth shook her head wearily. "I'm beat," she announced. "Please tell me you're here to take over for me."

"I am," Enid replied. "Maria sent me in. You know, that girl's amazing—you'd think she was the mayor of this town instead of her father."

"She will be someday," Elizabeth said. She told Enid how to use the list of home placements and, after giving Enid a quick hug, left the office. Elizabeth headed outside, weary all over. She needed a few moments of fresh air.

Elizabeth spotted Winston Egbert sitting on a picnic table on the community center's front lawn, and she sat down beside him, leaning against her skinny, goofy friend for support.

"It's pretty bleak in there, isn't it?" Winston said softly as he put his bony arm around Elizabeth. "Even I can't find anything funny about all this."

"Oh, please don't lose your sense of humor," she begged him.

"I think it's gone south for a while," Winston admitted glumly. "This is awful. I'm already so sad, and we still have to make it through Olivia's funeral on Wednesday. Are you ready for that?"

Elizabeth swallowed. Hearing Winston—the school clown—talk about a weighty subject like death felt deeply unsettling. "Of course not," she said softly. "Have you seen or talked to Ken?" Ken was one of Winston's best friends along with Todd. "Any idea how he's handling it?"

"I've called him," Winston replied with a sigh, "but his mother told me he doesn't want to talk to anybody. I can't imagine he's doing well, you know? I don't even want to think what I'd be going through if something had happened to Maria. . . ."

"Don't think about it," Elizabeth said, resting her head on Winston's shoulder. "Just count your blessings."

"I have been," Winston said sadly. "Believe me, I have been."

Jessica took a moment to compose herself behind a rack of donated clothing. She was shocked by all the misery in the room around her.

When she'd first arrived at the community center that morning, Jessica had asked Maria Santelli to give her something to do where she'd be out of the way. Maria had been so surprised that she'd asked Jessica to repeat herself twice. Usually Jessica craved the spotlight. But that was the old Jessica. The new, little-girl-killing Jessica couldn't care less about being the center of attention, and she'd been content to sort clothing all by herself in a back room.

But now all the clothes had been sorted, and Jessica found herself wandering around the basement, wincing as she saw the pain and despair on the faces of the people around her. *What chance do I have to pull my life back together,* she thought, *when someone way tough and cool like Dana Larson is over there waiting in the food line?* Dana was a punky girl who was also a student at SVH, and she was the lead singer of The Droids, the best band in town.

Mrs. Abernathy, the president of the PTA,

caught Jessica's eye and gave her a small smile. Jessica flinched. She was sure everyone could see the guilt over killing Alyssa written all over her face, and that made her feel as exposed as an open wound.

Maybe I should just leave, Jessica thought. But she didn't really want to leave. *Because I deserve to be miserable along with everyone else.*

In a weird way Jessica felt responsible for everything bad that had happened to all the people in the center. *I know it's crazy,* she realized, *but I can't help thinking that it's all my fault. Like my own shallow, selfish life brought down misery on the entire town, and now everybody has to pay for my stupid, frivolous existence!*

It had been a truly terrible idea to come to the community center. *I must've been deranged to think I could help anyone else,* Jessica thought. *I'm nothing but bad news.*

"OK," she whispered into the rack of clothing in front of her. "I'm outta here."

But just as Jessica was about to slip out the side door she heard someone say her name.

"There you are," Maria Santelli called over as Jessica froze in place. "I've been looking all over for you."

Jessica flinched as she saw that Maria was leading a little boy over to her. She had to fight the urge to flee. The little dark-haired boy was crying, and the sight of him made Jessica struggle

101

to keep from bursting into tears herself.

"This is Marcus Pontil," Maria told Jessica when she'd reached her. "He's eight years old."

Jessica just stared at the boy, trying hard to control her breathing, which suddenly seemed harsh and ragged.

Maria leaned over close to Marcus's ear. "Sweetie, I'll be right back, OK? Don't go anywhere."

Marcus nodded, tears still streaming down his face.

"Jessica," Maria said, "let me talk to you for a minute." Numbly Jessica allowed Maria to lead her a few steps away from Marcus. When they were out of earshot, Maria whispered, "Listen, Jess. His father—his only parent—is unconscious in the hospital and is in extremely critical condition. Marcus has no other family in Sweet Valley, and he's staying at our house for a while."

"That's terrible," Jessica muttered. She wanted nothing to do with Marcus—she didn't even want to look at him. The sight of his big, frightened eyes reminded her so strongly of Alyssa's that Jessica's stomach churned. "What does this have to do with me?"

"Watch him for a while, will you, Jess?" Maria asked. "Just play with him. I'm too busy, and I don't want to leave him alone."

"Uh . . . I was just leaving," Jessica protested. "I've got to get home to . . . to—"

"Great!" Maria told Jessica with a big smile. "I knew you'd help out." She turned around and called to the little boy. "Marcus, sweetie, come over here and meet Jessica."

Marcus obediently wandered over.

"No, wait," Jessica said. She simply could not handle this, not after what had happened with Alyssa.

"Jess, you're the best," Maria said. She stuck Marcus's hand in Jessica's and then rushed off.

"Maria!" Jessica called. But Maria didn't slow down for a second.

As soon as she was gone Marcus dropped Jessica's hand and wrapped his arms tightly around her leg. Jessica stared down at the little boy clinging to her. His nose was running, and his eyes and cheeks were streaked with tears.

Despite herself she reached down and tousled his wild shock of dark hair. "You're a mess, you know that?" she told Marcus.

He nodded, and Jessica sighed. She leaned over and rummaged through a box of clothing until she found a donated handkerchief she'd packed earlier. She quickly used it to clean Marcus's face. Jessica actually wasn't all that surprised that he'd stopped crying. For some reason she'd never fully understood, she'd always been good with kids. She'd been a baby-sitter countless times, a summer-camp counselor, and an au pair—and in almost every case the children had loved her immediately.

"Marcus, my man," Jessica said. "What shall we do to keep busy?"

Marcus smiled up at her and revealed a space where one of his baby teeth had fallen out. "I like puzzles," he replied.

"OK, puzzles it is," Jessica said. She opened a box of donated toys, managed to locate a jigsaw puzzle of a Saint Bernard, and handed it to Marcus. Then she sat down beside him on an old woven rug somebody had given to the center and they got started.

"Look, Jessica," Marcus announced when he had connected his first piece. "I made the eye!"

Jessica peered at the two pieces. "That's very good," she praised Marcus, "but it's important to try to put the edges together first."

"OK," Marcus said with a nod.

He returned his attention to the puzzle, and Jessica leaned back to watch. *He's a cutie,* she thought. *I really hope his father's going to be all right.*

Elizabeth slumped over in the passenger seat of her father's car and rested her head on the window. Enid was in the same position in the back, and Jessica was driving. Elizabeth was pretty sure she'd never felt so exhausted in her life.

Well, maybe when we were trying to outrace that flash flood in Death Valley, she amended. The twins and a few friends had spent a couple of days in the desert as part of a survival weekend, and the whole trip had turned out to be an endless series of disasters. *But that was* physically *draining,*

Elizabeth remembered, *and today has been* emotionally *exhausting*.

As Jessica drove through the streets of Sweet Valley, Elizabeth groggily noticed that after the last few days of intense cleanup, the town was already starting to look a little better. There were still signs of destruction everywhere—street signs knocked down, flattened houses, and big cracks in the roads. But the overturned cars had been moved, and most of the fallen tree limbs and telephone wires had been cleared away.

Elizabeth peeked at her twin. Jessica seemed a little better too. *She looks calmer,* Elizabeth decided. Maybe playing with that little boy all afternoon had restored some of her spirit. *See, helping out the town was good for us all,* she thought. Certainly Elizabeth didn't expect Jessica to make a full recovery for a long, long time, but any change in Jessica's bleak state had to be for the better. She had nowhere to go but up.

On their way back to Enid's house Jessica was forced to turn down Calico Drive. Jessica's expression grew grim as they neared their house, and her hands tightened on the steering wheel as she sped up. Elizabeth understood completely. She wasn't feeling particularly psyched to see their destroyed home again either.

She closed her eyes as Jessica zoomed past the house.

"Wait, wait, stop!" Enid cried. "Go back!"

Elizabeth looked up, and Jessica slowed down slightly. "What?" she asked. "What's wrong?"

"Devon," Enid replied, craning her neck to look out the back of the car. "I thought I saw his motorcycle in your driveway. Can we stop?"

"Jess?" Elizabeth asked.

"Whatever," Jessica said with a shrug. She backed up the car.

Sure enough, Devon's motorcycle was in the driveway. As soon as Jessica hit the brakes Enid climbed out and hurried over to Devon, who had just appeared from behind the edge of the house.

Elizabeth turned to her twin. "You coming, Jess?" she asked.

"Nah," Jessica replied, staring directly out the front windshield. "I'll wait here. Make it quick, OK?"

Elizabeth knew that Devon wasn't Jessica's favorite person—she'd made a major play for Devon's attentions when he'd first moved to town, but he'd only been interested in Elizabeth. The whole situation between Elizabeth, Jessica, Devon, and Todd had gotten very complicated, leaving all four of them hurt in different ways. "I'll hurry," Elizabeth promised.

As Elizabeth made her way over to where Enid and Devon were standing, she started to feel jealous. Enid's arms encircled Devon, and he was smiling weakly down at her, shaking his head at the lavish praise she was heaping onto him.

Enid's going way overboard, Elizabeth thought.

Why can't she figure out that she's doing nothing but embarrassing him by . . . by drooling all over him like that?

Elizabeth felt a little guilty for having such a petty thought about her best friend, but her guilt was immediately forgotten when Devon turned to look at her. Devon's slate blue eyes were so mesmerizing that they momentarily took her breath away. In his gray T-shirt and loosely hanging, beltless jeans Devon looked incredibly attractive.

"Hi, Elizabeth," Devon said as he turned away from Enid. "Before you ask, I'm at your house because—"

"So, why are you here at my house?" Elizabeth asked at the same time.

They both laughed nervously.

"I'm sure he has a good reason," Enid piped up.

Devon glanced quickly at Enid.

"You were saying?" Elizabeth prompted.

"Uh . . . I just stopped by to . . . ," Devon began, "um . . . to make sure my memories of what happened here matched up with the . . . reality."

Elizabeth could understand that—she knew plenty about shaky memories! "And?" she asked.

"Everything seems to be exactly the way I remembered it," he said.

"I wish I could say that," Elizabeth told him with a smile. "Everyone keeps telling me what went on after the earthquake, but it doesn't seem quite real to me, you know? It's like I'm reading about myself in a book or seeing it in a movie. It feels . . . detached."

"Maybe you should just try to forget about it," Devon suggested. "It wasn't that much fun to begin with. . . . There's no need to relive it."

"I wish I had been awake to see you rescue me," Enid told him. "I'm sure it was very exciting to watch you being so brave."

Ugh, Elizabeth thought. *Isn't that laying it on a bit thick?*

To Devon she said, "Still, I wish I could remember everything. Without a big chunk of my memories, I don't feel complete."

Devon nodded.

"Hey, Devon," Enid said. "How about giving me a ride on your motorcycle? If you're going home, that is. Your place is closer to mine. Liz and Jessica should be going in the opposite direction to get to Fowler Crest."

"Uh, sure," Devon replied. "I'll see you later, Elizabeth, OK?"

"OK," Elizabeth said. But really she didn't feel OK about it at all. She stood on her front lawn, watching for a moment as Enid raced over to Devon's bike and pulled on his extra helmet. Elizabeth started walking back to the car while Devon climbed on his Harley-Davidson and Enid slid on behind him, cinching her arms around his waist.

Elizabeth didn't approve of motorcycles. She'd seen enough accidents to know how dangerous they were. In fact, she herself had spent some time in a coma as a result of a motorcycle crash, and her cousin, Rexy, had been killed on one.

But it wasn't really the motorcycle that made Elizabeth squint in irritation at Devon and Enid as they rode away.

It was nothing but jealousy.

That should totally be me, Elizabeth thought hotly as she opened the car door. *What's Enid doing, trying to steal Devon?*

She dropped herself down on the seat and slammed the door. For a second she just stared at her hands, willing herself to calm down.

Why am I being such a baby? Elizabeth wondered. *Enid's my best friend! Anyway, I know for a fact that it's me Devon loves. He always has. There's no question about it.*

But if that was true, then why wouldn't the odd, churning ache in her stomach subside?

With a sigh Elizabeth turned to face her sister.

Jessica smiled and started the car, arching one eyebrow at Elizabeth. "Love's a bummer, huh?" Jessica asked.

"Yes," Elizabeth replied, closing her eyes. "It sure is."

Chapter 8

Devon squirmed as Enid slid her hand along his stomach muscles under the obvious pretense of getting a better grip. The geeky girl was getting just a little too friendly, but besides sending out massive uncomfortable vibes, Devon didn't know how to tell her to stop without insulting her. After all, she did need to hang on to avoid falling off the bike.

But if it had been Elizabeth behind him . . . now that would be a different story. Elizabeth would have been more than welcome to cling to him. Maybe she would even slip her hand under his shirt, her soft fingers touching his skin—

Devon revved his engine to cut that thought dead. The last thing he needed was to get all hot and bothered while someone like Enid was pressed up against him.

"So . . . !" Enid shouted, struggling to be heard over the wind. "What are your plans for the summer?"

"What?" Devon hollered. He'd heard her—he just didn't feel like making small talk.

"I asked what your plans were for the summer!"

"What?" Devon shouted again.

"The summer!"

Devon shrugged and pointed at the side of his helmet, indicating that he couldn't hear her. To his relief, Enid lapsed back into silence.

A few minutes later, as Devon roared down Ocean Avenue, Elizabeth once again invaded his thoughts. He wished he could have hung out with her longer. Every time they exchanged more than three words, he wanted nothing more than to be with her someplace totally private and enjoy a long conversation with her, face-to-face. Yes, Elizabeth was beautiful, but that wasn't the reason he'd fallen in love with her. She'd stolen his heart because every interaction with her was, like, a *symphony* of unspoken communication. There were so many levels to the connection they shared, and every moment he spent with her felt meaningful.

But of course I couldn't have hung out longer, he thought, *for two very good reasons.* First of all, Jessica had been there, glaring at him from the car. It wasn't that Devon was scared of Jessica—of course not. But he didn't mind admitting that he found her far too intense, and, well . . . formidable.

He'd always considered Jessica a disaster just waiting to happen, and he hadn't been at all surprised to hear that she'd gotten herself so badly damaged in a trauma with some girl. Generally when Jessica was around, Devon did his best to be someplace else.

The second reason he'd hightailed it away from the Wakefield house was his own guilt. *And I lied to Elizabeth again,* he realized. Of course he hadn't been at the house to check out the destruction and see if it matched up with his memories. That was a pretty lame excuse, and the only reason Elizabeth had bought it so easily was because she was trying to recover her own memories. No, he'd gone to Elizabeth's house hoping he could find something he could salvage for Elizabeth—something precious to her that would make up for his betrayal in his own mind. But after a few minutes of looking around, it had been pretty obvious that the Wakefields had already been there and had taken what they could.

Why did I ever accept the credit for saving her? he wondered. *How stupid was that?*

He sighed, overwhelmed with an emotion that he couldn't immediately identify. After a moment of thinking about it, he managed to put his finger on the strange, sickening emotion—he was *ashamed.* Ashamed of his own cowardice.

Devon slowed his motorcycle as the traffic light up ahead turned red. *Maybe I don't need to feel ashamed,* he told himself. It was an extremely unpleasant emotion. *After all, I did what I had to do to keep myself alive.*

Devon pulled the bike up to a stop behind a minivan at the red light. *I had to save myself— that's the most important thing,* he reassured himself. *And if Elizabeth thinks less of me when she finds out . . . well, then so be it.*

But Devon couldn't help wincing at the thought of Elizabeth's anger and scorn when—if—she ever did find out.

"Are you OK?" Enid asked.

Devon flinched. He'd almost forgotten she was there. "Yeah, sure," he replied, "I'm OK." The light changed, and Devon started up the road again, making a right turn at the second street.

Up ahead was his own house, which he had to pass in order to take the fastest route to Enid's place. Devon peered up the road through his visor—there seemed to be some sort of commotion in front of his house. What were all those lights in his yard? Why were there cars and vans blocking the street? And what was going on with all those *people?*

"Oh, no," Devon muttered, realizing what the crowd was. *They're reporters!*

He pulled up in front of his house with a screech.

"There he is!" a female reporter yelled. Instantly everybody swarmed around Devon's bike, pointing microphones and television cameras at him.

"Are you the guy who rescued the two girls?" a bald reporter demanded.

"How'd you find the courage to do something so dangerous?" a woman with red hair asked.

Another guy in a suit stuck a microphone up to Devon's helmet. "Were you sent to earth by aliens who control your mind?"

Devon flipped up his visor. "What is all this?" he asked, confused.

Behind him Enid pulled off her helmet. "Isn't it cool?" she whispered. "You're going to be famous!"

"No," Devon replied. "It's horrible." He flipped his visor down again, planning to wheel the motorcycle around and make a break for it.

"Hey, everybody!" Enid called, sliding off the bike. "This guy saved my life! He's my hero! Ask him about how he pulled me away from power lines that almost killed me!"

The red-haired woman held a small tape recorder up to Devon's visor. "Is that true?" she asked.

Devon's first thought was to say no, that he'd lied, that he'd made up the whole thing. He knew he should just come clean before this mess got completely out of hand.

But maybe it was already too late.

Because with dozens of microphones poking at his face and just as many video cameras staring at him, what was he really supposed to say?

* * *

Elizabeth carried a big ceramic bowl of buttered popcorn into the Fowlers' vast television room and sat down on an exquisitely comfy couch between her parents and Lila. Mrs. and Mr. Fowler shared a love seat nearby.

"Mmm, popcorn," Mr. Wakefield said. He grabbed a handful.

"It smells wonderful," Mrs. Fowler added as everyone in the room took a share. "But wherever did you get it, Elizabeth? I thought I gave the cook the night off."

"I *made* it," Elizabeth replied, a little snippily. Mrs. Wakefield shot her a "mind your manners" glance. "You have a beautiful kitchen," Elizabeth quickly told the Fowlers. "It's so . . . big."

Mrs. Fowler laughed. "I'm glad you like it," she said. "Why, I don't believe I've been in it myself for months now, since there was that mixup with the caterers. And I don't think George has *ever* been in it."

"Not true," Mr. Fowler said cheerfully. "I made myself a sandwich once—right after the last time Lila decided to fire the cook."

Mrs. Fowler smiled at her husband. Elizabeth knew that the Fowlers hadn't always been so happy in their marriage. In fact, they'd been divorced during most of Lila's childhood, and Mrs. Fowler had lived in France during that time. But after John Pfeifer had assaulted Lila, she had gone through a very dark period and had needed her mother. Not only had Grace Fowler returned home to help Lila, but she'd also reconciled with Mr. Fowler, and they'd gotten remarried in a large and elegant ceremony on the grounds of Fowler Crest. "Please, feel free to use the kitchen anytime you desire. Our house is your house," Mrs. Fowler told Elizabeth.

"Thank you," Elizabeth replied sincerely. She did become irritated occasionally with the Fowlers' rich, clueless lifestyle and their dependence on their servants, but they were very generous and warm hosts.

Lila yawned and curled her legs under her. "Where's Jessica?" she asked.

The Wakefields and the Fowlers had gathered after dinner to watch the local news together since the state of Sweet Valley was utmost on everyone's mind.

"Jessica said she was feeling tired after her long day," Mrs. Wakefield said in answer to Lila's question. "So she went up to bed early."

"Shhh . . . ," Mrs. Fowler murmured. "The news is starting."

Dyan Sutton appeared on the big-screen TV, announcing that she had a special report on the earthquake's aftermath.

"There's Dyan!" Mrs. Fowler said. "Doesn't she look good?" Dyan was Amy Sutton's mother and shared Amy's ash blond hair and cute, upturned nose. Mrs. Fowler and Mrs. Sutton were good friends. Mrs. Sutton had been WXAB's sports-caster for over a year.

117

"Amy said that Dyan got promoted," Lila muttered. "Amy hasn't shut up about it since she heard this morning. The usual guy broke his arm in the earthquake, so Dyan took over."

"How terrible," Mrs. Fowler said. "But how lucky for Dyan."

Elizabeth strained to hear what Mrs. Sutton was saying over the Fowlers' chatter. It was something about a story of heroism. . . .

She gasped as a picture of Devon on his motorcycle filled the enormous screen. Devon pulled off his helmet and grimaced at the camera.

"I *warned* Dyan about that blazer when she bought it with me," Mrs. Fowler said. "It does nothing for her coloring."

"Shhh!" Elizabeth hissed urgently. "That's Devon! That's the guy who saved me!"

The chatter in the room silenced as everyone turned their attention to the TV. ". . . and is credited with saving the lives of two Sweet Valley girls, Enid Rollins and Elizabeth Wakefield," Dyan Sutton was saying.

Elizabeth felt the blood rush to her face at the mention of her name.

"While he was at first reluctant to speak to reporters," Mrs. Sutton continued, "we finally convinced Devon Whitelaw to recount his story for us."

"Yeah, I pulled them away from the power lines," Devon said with a sigh.

"He doesn't seem very excited about it," Lila noted.

"One of the girls Devon rescued, Enid Rollins, was at the scene to give us her impressions too," Dyan Sutton said in a voice-over as the image changed to a shot of a smiling Enid.

"Devon's the bravest guy in the world!" Enid said enthusiastically to the camera. "I just can't thank him enough!"

"What a geek!" Lila said with a chuckle. "Will you check out that dress she's wearing? *Pathetic!*"

After all Enid's attention to Devon, Elizabeth wasn't in the mood to defend her. And the flower-print dress Enid was wearing was slightly dowdy; even Elizabeth had to admit that. Still, Enid was her best friend, so Elizabeth felt as though she should say something. "Enid didn't know she was going to be on television," she told Lila.

"There's no excuse for a dress that bad," Lila replied.

With a groan Elizabeth turned back to the TV. Her stomach dropped as she saw that the final shot of the special report was an image of Enid hugging Devon tightly. Elizabeth flared up with jealousy.

"What a nice report," Mrs. Wakefield said as the broadcast cut to a commercial. "I'm glad to see that Devon is getting the attention he deserves."

I shouldn't feel so jealous, Elizabeth reprimanded herself. *Enid is my best friend! I should be happy that Devon saved her life as well as mine.*

Besides, she told herself firmly, *Devon loves only me. He can't have forgotten our past.*

❖   ❖   ❖

119

Jessica smiled down at Marcus Pontil and squeezed his hand happily as the cute little boy returned her smile with a gap-toothed grin.

They were taking a stroll past the Sweet Valley library. It was late at night, and a strange mist was rolling in, making it a little hard to see. But Jessica tried to ignore the eerie atmosphere and concentrate on having a good time with Marcus. The little boy's father was gravely injured, and Jessica knew that cheering Marcus up was much more important than paying attention to her own fears.

Then a giant rumbling noise filled Jessica's ears. *No!* she thought, her heart lurching with terror. *Not again . . .*

But despite Jessica's pleas, the earth between herself and Marcus split and then yawned open as the ground rippled and shook. Jessica was knocked off her feet and landed hard on the asphalt in front of the library. She lost her grip on Marcus's hand.

Marcus screamed as he tumbled down into the fissure in the earth.

Jessica sat up in bed, covered in cold sweat. She struggled for breath as she reassured herself that it had only been a dream. Another in a terrible series of endless nightmares.

Marcus is fine, she told herself. *Alyssa died, not him.*

Tears streamed down Jessica's cheeks as her heart thudded in her chest. *Imagine,* she thought, *imagine how it would feel to die that horribly. . . .*

Oh, I'm so sorry, Alyssa! I'm so truly sorry!

Still Jessica couldn't catch her breath. The Fowlers' guest bedroom felt much too close and confining. She needed air. Fresh air.

Outside, she thought, her lungs clenching. *I need to get outside now.*

Jessica quickly scrambled out of bed, pulled on a jacket over her T-shirt and sweatpants, and slipped into a pair of sneakers. Then she left her room and hurried out of Fowler Crest through the side door in the west wing.

I have to find somewhere I feel safe, Jessica thought as she broke into a run over the estate's well-manicured lawn, taking deep gulps of the cool night air. *A place where I have only good memories—if such a place still exists.*

The phone rang in the Matthewses' living room.

Ken was lying on his side on the couch, and the phone was on an end table only a few feet from his head. But he didn't move to answer it. There was nobody he wanted to talk to.

At least nobody who was still alive.

Finally Ken's mother walked in and picked up the phone. "Oh, hello," she greeted the caller somberly. "I was so sorry to hear . . . ," she said, her voice trailing off as the caller spoke. "Yes, I'm sure it was. Oh . . . Yes, he's here. Please hold on a moment."

Mrs. Matthews held the phone out to Ken. "It's for you," she said.

Ken just shook his head no and closed his eyes.

Then he felt his mother's cool hand brush his cheek gently and he blinked, looking up into her worried face. "Please, honey," she said softly. "It's important."

Ken sighed and took the phone. "Hello?"

"Ken? This is Mrs. Davidson."

Ken sat up on the couch. "Hi," he said. "How are you?"

There was a shaky intake of breath. "As well as can be expected," she replied, her voice cracking slightly. She paused. "I'm sorry. Every time I think I'm OK to talk, I start to break down again." She took another deep breath. "How are you holding up?"

Ken thought about how to answer that question. To anyone else he would have answered coldly or refused to reply at all. But this was Olivia's mother. If anyone could understand the pain he was suffering, she could. "Pretty badly," he said. "I miss her all the time, you know?"

"I know," Mrs. Davidson said sorrowfully. "I can't believe how quiet this house is without her. I keep expecting to see—"

"To see her everywhere," Ken finished for her. "Me too."

Mrs. Davidson let out a soft sob, then fell quiet for a moment. Ken waited patiently for her to regain control, wishing there was something he could do for her. Ken himself was in no danger of tears. Over the past few days he had already cried himself out, and now he felt almost nothing but a hollow emptiness inside him. And guilt, of course, for his starring role in Olivia's death.

"Ken?" Mrs. Davidson asked, her voice sounding a little muffled. "You still there?"

"I'm here," he said.

"This isn't just a social call," she told him. "I have a favor to ask you."

"Yes?"

"You know we're planning a memorial service for Olivia on Wednesday in our backyard, right?" Her voice was gaining strength.

"Of course," Ken replied.

"Good," Mrs. Davidson said, sounding grateful. "My husband and I were hoping you'd be kind enough to give the eulogy, just a few words about how much Olivia meant to you. It doesn't have to be anything fancy. You can just say what's in your heart."

Ken moved the phone to his other ear. He felt honored—and shocked—by Mrs. Davidson's request. But most of all, he felt confused. On the one hand, he had loved Olivia more than anything in the world, and he knew it was his duty as her boyfriend to speak at her service. But on the other hand . . .

I'm responsible for her death, Ken thought morosely. *I failed in saving her. It wouldn't be right for me to speak.*

"Ken?" Mrs. Davidson asked. "What do you think?"

"I'm not sure—"

"Don't answer right away," Mrs. Davidson broke in. "Why don't you come over tomorrow so we can talk about it?"

"Tomorrow?" Ken repeated. "Uh . . . I don't know if—"

"Please," Mrs. Davidson said. Ken could tell she was close to tears again. "It would mean a lot to me and Mr. Davidson. Please."

"OK," Ken agreed. When asked like that, how could he say no? "What time should I stop by?"

"Around noon," Mrs. Davidson said. "I'll see you tomorrow, then?"

"See you tomorrow," Ken replied.

As he hung up the phone Ken looked up at his mother, who was standing behind the couch. "Mrs. Davidson wants me to give Olivia's eulogy," Ken explained.

"It's good to do that," Mrs. Matthews said. "It's a good way to say good-bye."

"Yeah?" Ken said. *Good-bye.* That word sounded so final . . . so *lonely.* A fresh wave of sadness washed over the numbness inside him, and Ken worked to swallow a sob. "I'm . . . I'm feeling really tired," he told his mother. "I think I'll go to bed early."

"Whatever you need to do," Mrs. Matthews replied.

Ken hugged his mother quickly and headed up to his room. But after he had turned off the light and settled into his bed, sleep wouldn't come.

Instead a memory of Olivia sifted up from his

subconscious to plague him. He saw her bone white face and the thin trail of blood that had streamed from her mouth as she lay dying under the Wakefields' refrigerator. Worst of all was the look of absolute love in her eyes as she had listened to Ken's promises to return with help. . . .

Ken gave up trying to sleep and headed down the hall to the bathroom. After washing his face he peered at his reflection in the mirror. He looked weary and miserable—even his perpetual tan had faded.

He leaned over the sink and closed his eyes, listening to Olivia's laughter echoing in his memory.

Tears started to run down Ken's cheeks, and he angrily wiped them away. Ken headed back to his room and quickly pulled on a pair of shoes. Then he hurried downstairs.

I can't stand being trapped with my memories for another minute, he thought as he left the house. He needed to get outside and *do* something. Maybe a long walk in the fresh night air would help him stop mentally beating himself up.

But Ken seriously doubted that anything would help. Because nothing could change the plain fact that the love of his life was dead.

Or the fact that he'd failed to save her.

Chapter 9

Jessica climbed the bleachers beside the Sweet Valley High football field and sat down in a row in the middle of the stands. With a grateful sigh Jessica saw that the stadium hadn't suffered any damage in the earthquake. In fact, the field looked oddly beautiful, the goalposts and gridiron lines glowing in the moonlight.

I was happy here, Jessica thought, wrapping her arms around her chest. So many of the best moments of her life had happened within this stadium. As she stared down at the dark field Jessica could almost imagine that she saw blurred, faint ghosts of her cheerleading squad bopping on the sidelines, getting ready to built a human pyramid and chanting rhymes to spur Sweet Valley High on to victory.

How many hours had she spent on this field,

during games or simply practicing with the squad? How many cute guys had she flirted with in these stands, and how many dance moves had she performed, boosting the fans' energy? It seemed like an infinite number in her memory—a countless amount of good times.

It's amazing, Jessica thought, *that being the star of the cheerleading squad actually* meant *something to me once.*

Because now, after Alyssa's death, all her wonderful memories of the games and cheers and cute jocks seemed dulled, like it had all happened to someone else. Someone who didn't know what pain and sadness truly were.

Who really cares about all those memories? Jessica wondered dejectedly. *Who cares that I was forced to accept Heather as my cocaptain? Who cares about the rivalries between the members of the squad for the attentions of Aaron Dallas or Bryce Fisherman? Who cares that all the students of Sweet Valley High once cheered along with words that I'd made up?*

Not Jessica. Not anymore. The only memory that still seemed valid was the time Nancy Swanson, the mousy adviser of the cheerleaders, had lost her mind and kidnapped the squad, planning to kill them because her brain was still stuck in the 1970s.

That's the truth about life, Jessica realized. *I wasted all my time wrapped up in stupid, trivial things, believing I was happy . . . when right around the corner, tragedy was always waiting to strike.*

I feel awful for Marcus, she thought, closing her eyes. *But at least that kid has learned an important lesson it took me seventeen years to figure out—that life is way harsh.*

As tears cascaded down her face from her closed eyes, Jessica imagined she could still hear the applause from the stands, the music of the marching band, and the booming voice of the sports announcer over the loudspeaker. *And now,* the announcer called in her mind, *please welcome to the field Sweet Valley High's own star quarterback, the captain of the Gladiators . . . Ken Matthews!*

Jessica sniffled, slumping down onto the bench. She couldn't help imagining that she was listening to the roars of the crowd as Ken hustled onto the field. The handsome blond quarterback would have waved to the excited fans in the bleachers as Jessica herself went into overdrive on the sidelines, shaking her pom-poms in the air.

Then she heard footsteps.

For a second Jessica kept her eyes closed, still thinking that she was only hearing the phantom sounds of her imagination. But the footsteps continued . . . and they were getting closer. She opened her eyes to look.

And there was Ken, climbing up the stands toward her. Was the sight of him only a product of her miserable mind? Had she finally gone around the bend?

No—in her imagination Ken hadn't looked nearly this depressed. He had dark circles under his eyes, and his usually cute tousled blond hair was now flat and limp.

Jessica just stared at Ken as he sat down beside her. Without a word he opened his arms and Jessica fell into his embrace, sobbing out all of her sorrow into his muscular shoulder.

This is where we are now, Jessica thought dismally. *The star cheerleader weeping in the arms of the star quarterback. As it should be.*

Because this is the reality of life.

Ken held Jessica as she cried. It felt really strange to be this close to her again—for the past few months he'd pretty much avoided hanging out with her if he could help it. Ever since their terrible breakup after she'd cheated on him, Ken hadn't wanted to deal with her, even though they'd been friends since kindergarten. *That all seems pretty pointless now,* Ken thought as he stroked her hair. It was hard to remember how badly Jessica had hurt him when the pain she'd caused was only a drop compared to the ocean of misery he was suffering now.

Finally Jessica calmed down somewhat and sat up. "What are you doing out here?" she asked, wiping her eyes.

Ken shifted, looking out at the field. "Oh, I couldn't sleep," he replied.

Beside him Jessica nodded and then rested her head against his shoulder. "Thinking about Olivia?" she asked softly. "I'm so sorry, Ken. I know how happy you two were together—"

"Yeah, I miss her—more than anything," he interrupted. "But it's all the guilt I'm feeling. . . ." Ken let his words trail off. How could he explain to Jessica the terrible burden he had to bear of being responsible for Olivia's death? She couldn't possibly understand.

"Guilt?" Jessica asked, sitting up straight. "Why?"

Ken clenched his hands into fists. "Because I *killed* her, that's why," he spat out. "There should have been something I could've done to save her. I failed her, and her death is all my fault."

Jessica didn't say anything, and after a moment Ken turned to face her. He was surprised to see an amazed expression on her face as she stared silently at him. "What?" he asked. "What's that look for?"

Jessica blinked and then shook her head. "It's just that . . . ," she began. "Well, that's exactly what I'm going through. *Exactly.* I'm sure you heard what happened to me with Alyssa Hewitt, the girl I—"

"I heard," Ken said, wincing a little as he recalled the details of Jessica's tragedy.

"Anyway," Jessica continued, "I've been totally beating myself up, thinking there had to be something I could have done to save her. I see Alyssa falling over and over again and hear myself promising I'd save her—"

"That's it!" Ken said. "That's what I'm doing. Remembering that I promised Olivia I'd return with help. But I was too late. By the time I came back, she was already . . . gone."

Jessica nodded sadly. "But Ken, listen to me," she told him. "It so wasn't your fault, really. The earthquake killed Olivia, not you. You did everything you could, but nothing would have helped."

"Yeah, maybe," he replied, wishing he could believe Jessica's words. "I could say the same thing to you too, you know. The earthquake killed Alyssa, not you."

Jessica swallowed and leaned her head against Ken's shoulder again. "It doesn't make it any easier, does it?" she whispered. "Everyone tells me it wasn't my fault. And in some deep part of my brain I know it was an accident. I *know* that. But I can't help thinking what it *means* to have a girl die right in front of you. It's like a *warning* somehow, you know?"

"What do you mean?" Ken asked.

"Like that I've been wasting my life," she replied. "It's like a warning that life isn't as fun as I thought it was."

"Yeah," Ken said. "I can see that."

"Somehow . . . ," Jessica whispered, "somehow both of us need to figure out how to accept that we both saw horrible accidents, and—"

"Forgive ourselves," Ken finished for her. "That's what we have to do, isn't it? Somehow we have to forgive ourselves."

Jessica nodded, rubbing her head against Ken's shoulder. "I guess," she said. "But how do we do that?"

They both fell silent. Ken wasn't sure he'd ever be able to think about Olivia's death and not have his stomach knot up with guilt. It was strange, though, how much Jessica seemed to take it for granted that Olivia's death was only an accident and that he'd done everything he could to save her. It was also very confusing that Jessica was going through such a similar thing. If Jessica wasn't responsible for Alyssa's death—and Ken believed that she wasn't—then what did that mean about his situation?

Maybe, he thought, *just maybe, there really was nothing I could've done to save Olivia—*

"You know what I keep thinking?" Jessica asked, interrupting his hopeful thought. "Sometimes I can't help thinking that it should have been me who died in Alyssa's place."

Ken stiffened. He felt himself welling up with unreasonable rage.

"That's such a lie!" he shouted at her, standing up.

"Ken," Jessica whined. "What are you—"

"Shut up!" he told her. "You have no right, no right at all, to be so . . . so self-pitying. So some kid died! You didn't even *know* her!"

"That doesn't matter!" Jessica protested. "If anything, that's worse—"

"Worse?" Ken thundered. "Worse? I lost Olivia—the love of my life! And you're trying to tell me that what happened to you is *worse?*"

All Ken's past resentments about Jessica resurfaced as she fell quiet. "Of *course* you don't understand true love," he told her spitefully. "Look at how . . . how *mercilessly* you cheated on me!"

Before Jessica could say anything, Ken bounded into the aisle and rushed down the bleachers, feeling a hundred times more miserable than he had before.

I thought Jessica Wakefield *could cheer me up? What a joke!*

Hot tears squeezed out of Ken's eyes as he ran toward home.

Jessica glared at Ken as he ran away. *How dare he suggest I've never known true love!* she thought hotly. *Just because I never loved* him!

Sure, she'd *liked* Ken a lot—and had enjoyed dating him. But he was definitely not one of the major loves of her life! Of all the guys she'd dated, only Christian Gorman—the guy she'd cheated on Ken with—and Sam Woodruff could really be considered true loves. Jessica had even dated A.J. Morgan for longer than she'd gone out with Ken . . . and she barely ever thought about A.J. anymore. A.J. hadn't been a true love, and neither was Ken.

Of course, both Sam and Christian had died in horrible accidents. *Like everything I love,* Jessica thought miserably.

In a way Ken was right—Jessica hadn't known Alyssa for more than a few minutes before she died. She'd never seen the girl before in her life. But that didn't matter. Alyssa's death had affected her in a way that Jessica simply could not handle. It had finally shown her how meaningless her entire life had been.

Jessica stood up and smoothed down her jacket where she'd been leaning on it. Then she took a deep breath and began to climb down the bleachers.

This is the lowest point of my entire existence, Jessica thought. *And if Ken can't realize that, then I guess we have nothing else to talk about.*

At the bottom of the stands she stopped and grabbed the top of the fence that surrounded the track. Jessica closed her eyes, trying to listen once again to the lingering echo of all the happy memories she'd had on the field—the same ones she'd heard before Ken had shown up.

But this time Jessica heard nothing but her ragged breath and the slow thump of her own beating heart.

What does Ken Matthews know anyway? she asked herself. *Who cares about him? Who cares about anybody?*

Who cares about life?

Chapter 10

"That was fast," Maria Slater said as she gave Elizabeth a big hug.

Elizabeth smiled at the striking, tall girl with close-cropped black hair. "First of all, I haven't seen you in days. And you can't just call and tell me there's something you need to talk about in person. I'm a maniac when I get curious," Elizabeth explained. "So . . . what's up?"

"Sit," Maria instructed.

Elizabeth plopped herself down on Maria's bed, settling herself back against the wall next to the lemon yellow curtains that framed the room's one window. Maria sat down on the other end of the bed, facing her.

"This is going to sound weird."

"Just *tell* me," Elizabeth ordered.

"Well, OK. When I was talking to Enid this

morning, she was babbling on about what a hero Devon was, right?"

"I've heard her doing that," Elizabeth said wryly. "It's a bit much, isn't it?"

"That's another topic entirely," Maria replied. "Anyway, she filled me in on your missing memories and the whole thing about Devon rescuing you two. Something about the story bothered me, though, and when I got off the phone with Enid, it started to bother me a lot."

"OK . . . ," Elizabeth said.

"I was knocked out for a while on your lawn after the earthquake, and when I was waking up, I overheard something."

"What?" Elizabeth demanded, leaning toward Maria.

"I'm pretty sure it was you and Devon arguing over rescuing Enid," Maria replied. "I couldn't catch all the words, but your voice sounded desperate, and he sounded . . . well, terrified."

"So?"

Maria shook her head. "Listen to me, Liz. I'm almost positive that Devon refused to help you! It sure sounded that way to me."

Elizabeth stared at her friend for a long moment. "No way," she said finally. "That's not what happened."

"Are you sure, Liz?" Maria asked. "I mean, how can you know? All I'm saying is that I heard Devon refusing to help you."

Elizabeth sat up straight. "You must have heard wrong," she said.

"I don't think so."

"You must have!" Elizabeth said, her voice rising. "Devon told me what happened. And I believe him. Of *course* I believe him. He's . . . he's my hero!"

"Liz," Maria said, "I'm just telling you what I heard. I would have come and helped you myself, but when I woke up, I couldn't see anything through all the smoke. And then I heard Ken calling for help from the house—"

"There's no way," Elizabeth said, standing up. "You must be remembering it wrong. You were knocked out. It must have messed up your memory."

Maria crossed her arms over her chest. "*You're* the one who can't remember what went down, not me," she replied tersely. "And honestly, I'm more than a little offended that you don't believe me."

"It just doesn't make any sense!" Elizabeth protested.

With a sigh Maria leaned back on her bed. "Girl," she said, "believe what you want to believe, but I know Devon did not save Enid. Or you."

"I'm outta here," Elizabeth snapped. "Why don't you call me when you start making sense?"

"Fine," Maria said.

"Good," Elizabeth replied. "And good-bye."

Elizabeth hurried downstairs and out of the

Slaters' house, steaming. *How dare Maria try to smear Devon's heroic, brave, loving actions?* she thought hotly. *There's no way what she told me could be true.*

Elizabeth peeled out of the driveway and turned the car toward Fowler Crest, bewildered by Maria's story. Besides Enid, Elizabeth considered Maria to be her best friend, and for as long as Elizabeth had known her, Maria had always been rational and levelheaded. She'd often provided sane, reasonable opinions when Elizabeth had felt particularly confused. And although Maria's earthy sense of humor could sometimes sting, Elizabeth had never noticed a malicious bone in her body.

So what's gotten into her now? Elizabeth wondered. *It's just so unlike Maria to make stuff up!*

"Watch," Jessica instructed Marcus. The little boy stared at her with his big brown eyes as she reached back with her arm and threw a stone, sending it skipping over the surface of Secca Lake. The small stone made five hops across the water.

"Cool," Marcus said. "My turn!" He picked up a rock and imitated Jessica. The rock skipped only once before settling into the lake with a loud plop.

But it was good enough for Marcus. "Did you see that, Jessica?" he asked with a big smile. "I did it!"

"You sure did," Jessica replied. "Keep going. I'm

sure you'll be an expert in no time if you practice."

As Marcus bent over to collect more rocks Jessica smiled at him. She was glad Maria had asked her to spend some time with him.

He really needed some fresh air out here in the park, Jessica thought. *And so did I.*

Although Secca Lake was still beautiful, the large state park around the central tree-lined body of water was pretty beat up from the earthquake. The recreation lodge near the entrance had fallen down, many trees had toppled, and a few angry-looking fissures had opened up in what used to be pristine, lovely parts of the ranger-patrolled grounds.

I've had so many good times here, Jessica remembered as she looked around the park. Just over a rise to the east was the rough dirt-bike trail where she'd first met Sam Woodruff at a race between Michael Harris and Artie Western. And then there had been Jessica's secret romantic meetings with Todd Wilkins right here by the lake. . . .

Wow, Jessica thought, blushing at the memory. *What would Liz do to me if she ever found out that Todd made a special trip to Sweet Valley to see me after he'd moved to Vermont?* Jessica knew the answer to that question— Elizabeth would never forgive her. Luckily the only place Jessica had confessed that particular secret was in her diaries, and Elizabeth was far too respectful of other people's privacy to read them.

Besides her dates with Sam and Todd and countless other boys at Secca Lake, there also had been barbecues, parties, and camp-outs with her friends and picnics with her family to remember fondly.

But even Secca Lake had its dark side.

How could Jessica forget that the racing track where she had met Sam was now the place where the annual Sam Woodruff Memorial Dirt Bike Rally was held? Jessica had organized it herself in Sam's memory as a fund-raiser for Students Against Drunk Driving.

Hidden behind the lighthearted life I led, there was always so much sadness, Jessica realized. *How was I ever stupid enough to believe that life was good?*

For a moment Jessica was struck with the horrid urge to leave Marcus on the shore and swim out to the deepest part of the lake. Once she was out there, she could just let herself sink. The water would close up over her head, and it would be like drifting off to sleep as the water filled her lungs.

There would be no more guilt and sorrow. There would be no more wondering about the point of life. She would drown, and all her pain would end.

As an eerie calm fell over her Jessica found herself tempted by the idea. Very tempted.

"Jessica?"

She blinked, trying to focus in on Marcus's face. "Yeah?" she asked flatly.

"Can you take me to see my father in the hospital soon?"

The lost, sad sound of Marcus's voice snapped Jessica out of her disturbing reverie. She reached out and pulled Marcus to her, holding him close.

Jessica wasn't sure how she should answer the little boy. She knew that Mr. Pontil was not expected to regain consciousness—and that would be incredibly rough for Marcus to handle. *But maybe it would be best if Marcus had a chance to say good-bye,* she thought. *And maybe, just maybe, Mr. Pontil will actually get better. . . .*

"Can you take me?" Marcus asked again. "I really want to go see him."

"Yes," Jessica replied. "Sure, I'll take you."

It wasn't that Jessica still believed in miracles— after what she'd been through recently, only a fool would still keep wishing on a star.

I just can't fail Marcus like I failed Alyssa, Jessica realized as she ran her hand through the little boy's soft dark hair.

I still have to try.

"Am I late?" Ken asked.

Mrs. Davidson shook her head and offered him a weak smile. That smile reminded him so strongly of Olivia's own that Ken had to struggle to keep from breaking into tears and running back to his car. Her mother even shared Olivia's deep hazel eyes. "Oh, Ken," Mrs. Davidson said, gesturing at him to follow her into the house, "I'm so glad you came."

Ken took a deep breath and allowed Mrs. Davidson to lead him into her sunny kitchen, where they joined Mr. Davidson at a circular table.

"Hello, Ken," Mr. Davidson said as Ken sat down beside him. "It's good to see you again."

Ken searched Mr. Davidson's face for signs that he was telling the truth. He couldn't imagine that if he'd just lost his daughter, he'd be particularly happy to see her *boyfriend,* of all people. How could the Davidsons look at him and stop themselves from being reminded that their daughter was dead? Especially since they must be secretly blaming him for not being able to save Olivia. But Mr. Davidson reached out and patted Ken on the shoulder, and there seemed to be nothing but warm affection for Ken in his sad green eyes.

"Would you like some juice?" Mrs. Davidson offered. As she opened the refrigerator and peered inside, Ken noticed she was shaking. "We've got apple, orange . . . and we still have some of that tomato concoction that Olivia loved." She looked up at Ken, and tears were shining in her eyes. He swallowed, unable to bear seeing her in so much pain. "I don't like the taste of it, but I just can't bring myself to throw it away," she said weakly.

"I'd love some apple juice," Ken replied

quickly. "If it wouldn't be any trouble."

Mrs. Davidson seemed to be happy to have something to do with herself. As she opened a cabinet and pulled out a glass Mr. Davidson cleared his throat.

"We've been busy all day making the final arrangements for the memorial service tomorrow," Mr. Davidson told Ken, rubbing his weary eyes with both hands. Ken realized they had probably slept even less than he had. "We're trying to do something that Olivia would have approved of. Unfortunately I don't share my daughter's talent for art and design, so I doubt we can pull off anything as *colorful* as she would have done."

Ken glanced at a notebook on the table, but he was unable to decipher any of Mr. Davidson's scrawl. "I'm sure whatever you do will be good," Ken assured him. "Olivia was very . . . nonjudgmental about other people's stuff unless she had to be for school or whatever."

"So true," Mrs. Davidson said as she handed Ken a glass of apple juice and sat down next to him.

"Thanks," Ken said. The juice was cold, and he gulped it greedily. His throat had become dry as he'd listened to Mr. Davidson speak about the memorial service.

"So, Ken, have you decided what you're going to say during your eulogy?" Mr. Davidson asked.

Ken stared at his glass of juice. He hated to

disappoint them, but he'd made his decision. "I thought about it for a long time," he said, "but it just doesn't feel right for me to speak at the funeral."

"What?" Mrs. Davidson covered her mouth with one hand. She choked back a sob. Ken's heart twisted in his chest.

Mr. Davidson covered his wife's free hand with his own. "May I ask why?"

"It just doesn't feel . . . right," Ken repeated, desperate to find better words to explain himself. "I shouldn't be the one to speak."

"I can't think of anyone better than you," Mr. Davidson said. Mrs. Davidson was sobbing quietly. She got up from the table, grabbed a tissue, and wiped her face. Mr. Davidson looked up at her, obviously concerned. Ken felt horrible for adding to their misery.

"Is it nerves?" Mr. Davidson asked. "It's very common to be afraid of speaking before large groups, but you shouldn't let that stop you. You'll be among friends."

"No, it's not that I'm nervous," Ken replied. "I just . . . can't, that's all."

"I think Olivia would have wanted you to," Mrs. Davidson said softly.

Ken reddened and looked down at his hands. "I don't think so."

Mrs. Davidson dropped back into her chair and faced Ken. Her face was a damp mask of pain. "I don't understand this. I thought you'd jump at the chance."

Ken couldn't take it anymore. "I left her," Ken choked out. "When she was trapped . . . under the refrigerator, I left her there. I went to get help, but I didn't come back fast enough. And when I did come back, she was already . . . she was already—"

"Don't tell me you're holding *yourself* responsible," Mr. Davidson broke in.

Ken could only nod.

"Oh, honey," Mrs. Davidson said. She got up from her chair and wrapped her arms around Ken's shoulders. "Nobody blames you. Not at all."

Ken had to fight back tears. "I blame myself," he whispered.

"Ken," Mr. Davidson said. "Listen to me. It was an accident. I wish more than anything that it hadn't happened. . . . I lie awake at night wishing that. But it was an accident, and that's all."

"No," Ken said. He had to press his lips together to keep a sob from escaping. "No, it was all my fault. There had to have been something more I could have done. If I'd been stronger or faster—"

"Ken, stop this," Mr. Davidson interrupted. "Stop attacking yourself. That will not bring Olivia back to life. Do you hear me? Olivia loved you. She *loved* you."

"We knew it from the way she spoke about you," Mrs. Davidson added, returning to her chair. "Which she did all the time."

"Constantly," Mr. Davidson said firmly. "We know she'd want you to speak for her at her memorial service."

"I can't," Ken replied, squeezing shut his eyes. "I just can't. Please don't make me."

For a long moment the three of them sat at the table in silence. Ken gripped his hands into fists, trying to surface above the tide of sadness that had engulfed him. *Olivia loved me,* Ken thought as he exhaled a long ragged breath. *Even her parents knew how much she loved me. How could I have failed to save a girl who loved me so much?*

"I've got an idea," Mrs. Davidson said slowly, breaking the silence. "Before you decide, why don't you spend a little while alone in Olivia's studio? It might help you sort out your feelings."

Ken opened his eyes but didn't look up at either of Olivia's parents. "I don't think I could handle that."

"Well, I think it's a good idea," Mr. Davidson said. "I don't mean to sound too much like a father, but I think I should even insist on it."

"Please, Ken?" Mrs. Davidson said wearily. "Just for a little while. It will be good for you, you'll see."

With a sigh Ken realized that there was really no way he could refuse. He knew that Olivia had loved her parents, and it was easy to see why. Oh, they were still parents, and as pushy as any adult could be. But Ken could see that all their efforts were based on kindness and on the deep love for their daughter that he had felt too. He just couldn't say no to the two people who had loved Olivia as much as he had.

"I'll go into the studio," he conceded. "But when I come back, you have to accept my decision no matter what it is. Is that fair?"

"Fair enough," Mr. Davidson agreed.

"Good," Mrs. Davidson said, wiping her eyes one last time. "I think you're doing the right thing."

Ken nodded and stood up, ready to be shown to Olivia's studio. What did it really matter if he did this for the Davidsons? It would make them happy. And right now they needed all the happiness they could get.

But Ken was sure his answer still would be a big, fat *no* afterward.

Jessica led Marcus through the halls of Joshua Fowler Memorial Hospital toward the reception desk. It was difficult to navigate the halls—the hospital was teeming with people who had been injured in the earthquake. The families of patients lined the corridors, talking in low voices as doctors and nurses rushed around in response to urgent messages over the loudspeaker. Jessica kept Marcus close to her as she sidestepped to avoid a group of orderlies pushing a gurney.

"Where's my dad?" Marcus asked.

"Hold on. I'll find out," Jessica replied.

She stepped up to the reception desk, planning

to ask if it was OK to bring Marcus in to see his father. But when the desk clerk turned around to face Jessica, her eyes widened in surprise.

"What?" Jessica asked, looking down at herself.

"Oh, I'm sorry," the young, harried-looking clerk replied. "I just didn't expect to see you back here so soon."

"Excuse me?" Jessica asked.

"Weren't you just in here a few days ago, recovering from an electrocution?"

"Oh, no," Jessica said, offering the clerk a weak smile. "That was my twin, Elizabeth. People get us mixed up all the time."

"Twins," the clerk breathed. "It's an amazing resemblance. Is your sister all right? Do you need some assistance?"

"No, no," Jessica said quickly. "I'm here for something else. Could you please tell me the room number of—"

"Oh, I almost forgot," the clerk interrupted. "Hold on a moment, won't you?" She disappeared behind the counter, then bobbed up again, holding a large plastic bag. "These are your twin's clothes," she explained. "Elizabeth Wakefield, right? She accidentally left them behind when she was admitted here the other day. I was just going to call your family to see if you wanted to come pick them up. But now you can take them."

"Sure, I guess," Jessica said, taking the bag. "*Anyway*, I was hoping Marcus here—" she indicated the little boy beside her—"could stop in and visit his father."

"Let me see," the clerk replied. "What's his father's last name?"

"Pontil," Jessica answered.

"Pontil?" the clerk asked, seeming startled. "That's Marcus Pontil?"

"Yeah," Jessica said. The clerk's reaction scared her. "What's the matter?"

"We've been calling over to Mayor Santelli's house all day, trying to reach him," the young woman replied.

"That's my fault," Jessica said, feeling panic rising in her chest. "I had him with me at Secca Lake. Is there a problem? Is everything OK? Is Mr. Pontil—"

"Come with me," the clerk broke in. "This way. Quickly!"

Jessica grabbed Marcus's hand and pulled him along with her as she hurried after the young woman. Her heart was thumping rapidly. If Marcus had missed saying good-bye to his father because Jessica had kept him too long at Secca Lake, she'd never be able to forgive herself! Jessica followed the clerk down a long corridor, fearing the worst.

The clerk stopped in front of room 16 and motioned for Jessica and Marcus to enter. Jessica started to shake. She peered around the curtain that shielded the bed from view, knowing with dread certainty that she would see that Mr. Pontil was . . .

Smiling.

Jessica gasped. She stared at the thirty-something man in the hospital bed, her mouth gaping open. He was sort of handsome, with dark hair just like Marcus's and sparkling brown eyes. He was awake, sitting up in bed, and he seemed fine.

"Dad!" Marcus called. The little boy dropped Jessica's hand and rushed toward the bed, throwing himself into his father's arms.

"Are you OK?" Marcus asked his father. "Are you all right now?"

"I'll be fine, champ," Mr. Pontil replied. "I'll be just fine."

Jessica grinned at the wonderful father-and-son reunion taking place in front of her.

Maybe, she thought, *in the middle of all the horror and harshness of life, miracles still do happen every now and then.*

Chapter 11

Elizabeth was just leaving one of Fowler Crest's upstairs bathrooms when Lucinda found her.

"Miss Elizabeth," the skinny maid said with painful politeness, "you have a visitor. A Miss Maria Slater is waiting in the front parlor. Would you like to greet her there or in another room?"

"The parlor will be just fine, Lucinda," Elizabeth replied.

"Should I tell Miss Maria that Miss Elizabeth will be right down?" Lucinda asked.

Elizabeth laughed. "I'll go down now. Thanks, Lucinda."

Elizabeth was glad that Maria had shown up to see her—especially if it meant she'd had a change of heart about Devon. *So close to Olivia's funeral,* she thought, *we should be sticking together, not arguing.*

Elizabeth opened the heavy wooden door to the front parlor and stepped inside. Maria was sitting on a light green love seat, and she looked entirely comfortable in the rich surroundings. But then, Maria always seemed comfortable wherever she was.

Maria stood up languidly, brushing down the funky black skirt she was wearing. "Before you say anything," she told Elizabeth, "let me apologize, OK?"

"Don't worry about it," Elizabeth replied as both girls sat down again on the love seat. "I hated fighting with you. I shouldn't have overreacted."

Maria looked surprised. "So you're actually considering that what I said about Devon might be right?"

"No. I still think Devon saved me," Elizabeth assured her. "But I realized that you were only trying to help."

"I was," Maria agreed with a smile. "It must be so frustrating not to be able to remember anything that happened."

"You have no idea," Elizabeth replied. "It's driving me crazy."

"OK, then," Maria said. "I think I know a way you can get your memories back. And then you won't have to take my word for what happened . . . *or* Devon's."

"How?" Elizabeth asked eagerly.

"You have to promise to try to keep an open mind."

Elizabeth groaned. "Are you going to tell me your plan or not?"

154

Maria adjusted the short, delicate scarf she was wearing around her neck. "This is going to sound really weird, but . . . well, what do you think of hypnosis?"

"Hypnosis?" Elizabeth replied. "You want to *hypnotize* me? Do you know how to *do* that?"

"Sure," Maria answered lightly. "Well, I think so anyway. Do you remember that guy I told you about, the one I dated when I lived in New York—Michael Winter? He was so cute but ultimately just way too weird. But he was a freshman at NYU, studying psychology . . . and he was totally into hypnotizing everyone. Like, he went around asking random people if he could put them into a trance. It eventually just got on my nerves, you know?"

"Freaky," Elizabeth said.

"Definitely," Maria agreed. "That was Michael in a nutshell—cute but freaky. Anyway, I saw him do it enough times that I should be able to put you under if I try. It's not dangerous in the least . . . I think."

"That's not very reassuring," Elizabeth said, shifting uncomfortably on the love seat.

"Do you want to remember or not?" Maria asked.

"Yeah," Elizabeth replied quickly. "More than anything. OK, let's give it a shot. But I'll bet you, if I do remember anything, it'll just prove that Devon saved me."

"You're on," Maria agreed. "Let me see your watch."

"You're really going to use a *watch?*" Elizabeth asked. "As in, *you are getting sleepy . . . you are getting sleepy . . . ?*"

"You've been watching too many old movies," Maria said. "No, I just want to know what *time* it is. So we'll know when we started this."

"Oh," Elizabeth replied, feeling a little foolish. She quickly looked at her wristwatch. "It's two-forty."

"Good," Maria said. "OK, now . . . just sit back, relax, and close your eyes."

Elizabeth did as Maria instructed. "Now what?"

"Shhh . . . ," Maria told her softly. "Now, really relax. Just let everything go—all your worries. Just imagine a dark, empty field in your mind."

"OK," Elizabeth said.

"Don't talk," Maria urged. Her voice had dropped to a husky whisper. "Now imagine you see a long staircase, and picture yourself standing at the very top. I'm going to start counting back from ten, and every time I say a number, I want you to blink once and imagine that you've taken a step down the staircase. With every blink I want you to feel your eyes getting heavier and heavier. When I say the number zero, you'll have reached the bottom of the staircase, and then you'll tell me what you remember. Are you ready?"

Elizabeth nodded. She was already feeling a little sleepy. All the emotional ups and downs of the past few days had taken their toll, and reclining on the love seat in the warm, stuffy parlor with Maria whispering to her was making her feel drowsy.

"Good," Maria told her softly. "You're doing great. Here we go. Ten. Blink slowly, and take a step down the staircase."

The staircase Elizabeth was picturing looked very similar to the one in the Fowlers' front hall, but this one only had ten steps. She imagined herself moving to the ninth step.

"Your eyelids are getting heavier," Maria intoned, "and your body feels warm, calm, and limp. You haven't felt this relaxed in ages, as though you were sinking into a tub of hot water. Nine. Take another step and slowly blink as you relax even more."

How could she be walking down a staircase *and* sinking into a tub of water at the same time? Maria continued to whisper.

"Your eyelids are getting even heavier," Maria said. "All your muscles are relaxed. Eight." She paused. "Seven. You feel wonderful, perfectly relaxed. All your tension has seeped out of you. Six."

Elizabeth began to drift off and had to struggle slightly to hold the image of herself descending the staircase in her mind. *Even if this doesn't work,* she thought, *it feels really good to relax for a while. . . .*

"Five," Maria whispered. "You're halfway down now, and you almost feel like you're floating."

It does feel like floating, Elizabeth thought. *I feel so sleepy. . . .*

"Four."

A lovely warmth spread over Elizabeth's body.

In her mind's eye she pictured herself stepping down to the third-to-last stair. The movement was so effortless, she felt as if she were melting down the stairs.

"Three."

Maria's voice seemed to echo from somewhere far above.

"Two," she whispered.

"One."

On the edge of the final stair Elizabeth looked down and saw a deep pool of dark water. It didn't frighten her at all. Instead it looked warm and inviting and indescribably peaceful. She was ready for Maria's voice to let her know she was allowed to take the plunge into that heavenly darkness.

"Zero."

Elizabeth snapped awake, her eyes popping open. She turned to find Maria staring at her with wide eyes. "Oh," Elizabeth said groggily. "I guess it didn't work."

Maria looked surprised. "What do you mean?" she asked.

Elizabeth sat up straight. "I mean, nothing happened."

Maria smiled. "Check your watch," she suggested.

As Elizabeth peeked down at her wristwatch she gasped. It was now 3:10. Even if she allowed ten minutes for the imaginary walk down the staircase, that still meant she'd been unconscious for nearly twenty minutes! "But I . . . ," Elizabeth stammered. "I don't remember anything! What happened?"

Maria gave her a quick hug. "You talked," she said. "I know it sounds impossible, but you were talking in this really low voice the whole time. I've never seen anyone go under as easily as you. Michael would've been amazed."

Elizabeth blushed. "What . . . what did I talk about?"

"At first you talked about Todd," Maria replied, leaning back into the love seat and crossing her long legs.

"Todd? Oh, no, what did I say—"

"It's cool," Maria said. "Don't worry, it wasn't anything embarrassing. Or not too embarrassing anyway. You really can't remember anything you said?"

"Not a word." Elizabeth shook her head. "So, c'mon, fill me in."

"Well, you were babbling something about Rick Andover and begging Todd to help you. And then you said something about Kelly's bar. And then you said, 'Not this time, Jess. It's my turn,' and you made weird kissing sounds. It all made *no* sense to me, Liz. Who's this Rick character? And when did you ever go to that awful Kelly's Roadhouse?"

Elizabeth laughed. "I didn't really," she said. "Oh, man, it's a long story—one I haven't thought about in *ages*. Rick was such a total jerk! Suffice it to say that the night I guess I told you about was the night I sort of won Todd away from Jessica . . . and it was the first night I really kissed him."

"Really?" Maria asked. "Wow . . . you went way back."

Elizabeth was amazed. There was no way Maria could have known about the events outside Kelly's Roadhouse at the beginning of the school year— Maria had still lived in New York then. *The hypnosis really must have worked,* she thought.

For a moment Elizabeth wondered why she had remembered a story about *Todd,* of all people. She didn't like the idea that hypnosis had brought out a memory of him, especially since thinking about Todd *consciously* still caused her to feel a twinge of pain. *But I suppose that he and I have a lot of history together,* she reasoned. *There's no denying the fact that Todd and I did date for a long, long time.*

Now, though, Elizabeth was pretty sure she was ready to move on. And she knew just the boy who just might be able to make her forget Todd Wilkins forever. "So . . . ," Elizabeth said, trying to sound nonchalant, "did I remember anything about the earthquake? Did Devon rescue me or not?"

"I was getting to that," Maria replied. "You're going to have to help me with this stuff too because it doesn't seem to make any sense. Anyway, after you rambled about Todd for a few, I steered you toward the earthquake—"

"How'd you do that?" Elizabeth wanted to know.

"Easy," Maria said with a short laugh. "I asked you, 'Liz, do you remember anything about the earthquake?'"

Elizabeth laughed along. "And what did I say?"

"Well, you were quiet for a while, and your face went through all these weird contortions." Maria demonstrated, scrunching up her face as if she were being tickled. "Then you started muttering something about a snake . . . and then you whined about falling into water. *Then* you complained about how impossibly heavy Enid was. What do you make of all that?"

"Not much," Elizabeth said, feeling totally confused. "I've had this feeling that a snake is important somehow, but I just can't figure out why. I didn't say anything else about it?"

"Not that I could tell," Maria replied. "*The snake, the snake,*'" she moaned, imitating Elizabeth's voice. "And that was it."

A chill ran up Elizabeth's spine at the sound of Maria copying her moan. But it didn't make any more sense than it had before.

"I don't remember falling into any water either . . . although I *did* have an image of a dark pool right before you said zero. Maybe I was talking about that."

"Possibly," Maria said.

"Devon did say I was pulling Enid away from the power lines for a while," Elizabeth mused. "Maybe that's why I was complaining that she was heavy."

"Supposedly he was *helping* you pull her," Maria pointed out. "Didn't he say that each of you took one of her arms? She wouldn't be that heavy then. Maybe he didn't help you after all."

"Of course he did," Elizabeth said grouchily. The memories she'd recalled under hypnosis were so annoyingly vague! The new pieces of the puzzle seemed to add up to exactly nothing.

Maria groaned and rubbed her eyes. "Liz, what makes you so sure? Why are you so ready to give him the benefit of the doubt?"

"It's simple," Elizabeth said, looking seriously into Maria's eyes. "I love him. And there's no way I would ever fall in love with a guy capable of lying to me that . . . that *horribly.*"

"Whatever you say," Maria replied.

"No," Elizabeth said firmly. "It's just not possible."

Ken wandered slowly through Olivia's studio, which took up the entirety of the Davidsons' garage. The last time he was here, Olivia had shown him the nude portrait she'd painted of him and he'd flipped out. Ken wished he could take that moment back. He wished he could have them all back.

It was a busy room. *As busy as Olivia's amazing brain,* Ken thought. There were canvases everywhere, stacked along the walls and hanging on every available surface. In the far corner was an easel covered with a sheet beside a long table strewn with coffee cans full of brushes and jars of paint. Small sculptures were scattered around the room, and there was a messy pottery wheel next to a large mound of thick red clay. A group of bean-bag chairs rested beneath a bookshelf lined with art books against the back wall.

Ken could barely bring himself to look at any of her artwork closely. He sat down on one of the bean-bag chairs, staring glumly out into the wild room.

I know what Mr. and Mrs. Davidson were trying to do, he thought. *They figured that if I saw her art, I'd realize how much I missed her and how incredible she was . . . and then I'd decide to speak at her service. But that's not going to happen.*

Because Ken already knew how incredible Olivia had been. And how could he forget how much he missed her? He felt it every moment of every day since she'd . . . gone.

Ken picked up a small magazine that was lying on one of the beanbags and felt a little jolt of surprise. It was a copy of *Visions,* the literary-art magazine that Olivia had founded at SVH. He idly flipped through it, glancing at the drawings and poems that the students had submitted. After a moment Ken put it back down. It probably would be pretty interesting if he weren't feeling so melancholy, but he wasn't in the mood to deal with it.

As he shifted in his beanbag chair he spotted Olivia's acoustic guitar leaning against the wall by the window. He reached out and pulled it into his lap, strumming the strings. He had no idea how to play guitar, but that was OK—Olivia hadn't really been very good at it either. He smiled as he pictured Olivia plucking at the strings, singing along in her low, husky, slightly off-key voice. She probably practiced the guitar in the very spot where Ken was sitting now.

That thought gave him the creeps, so he put the guitar down and rose to his feet. *I guess I might as well look around,* he decided. *I know it's not going to help, but it can't hurt anything either.* Besides, he had always been curious about what Olivia had been doing during the long hours she spent alone in her studio.

Ken headed toward a group of beach landscapes hanging on the wall. The scenes were painted with heavy, thick brush strokes, and the colors were wacky—a yellow ocean, blue sand, all under a bright red or green sky. They seemed to pop right out from their canvases, and Ken couldn't help enjoying the turbulent feelings they brought out in him.

Near the seascapes was a large painting that seemed to be really different from anything else in the room. It was a picture of a kitchen, done very realistically, and there was a woman sitting at a table far in the background. It didn't look like anything Olivia would have done. For a second Ken shook his head, amazed at Olivia's range, but then he noticed the signature in the corner. *S. Bachman,* the signature read. Olivia hadn't painted it after all—it had been done by Stuart Bachman, who had been Olivia's art teacher.

Ken narrowed his eyes at the painting, suddenly feeling a twinge of jealousy. Olivia had confessed to Ken that she'd had a massive crush on Stuart when he'd been her teacher. Of course, Olivia had also said that she was completely over him—especially since Stuart had gotten married. But the Bachman was still a little too prominently displayed for Ken's liking.

Annoyed, he turned away from the paintings on the walls and headed over to a shelf lined with smaller sculptures near the door.

He stared at a small clay horse for a little while. He liked the way Olivia had captured the bunching of the horse's muscles as it ran. Next to the horse was a plaster sculpture of a pair of clasped hands. Ken had just decided that he liked the hands a lot—the fingers were so realistic and strong— when he spotted the title of the piece inscribed in the base. *Harry's Hands,* it was called.

Ken grimaced. Harry Minton was a guy who Olivia had dated before him. The last thing he wanted to be doing was admiring a sculpture of the hands of one of her exes. As Ken turned away he felt even more jealous than he had before.

Like I needed to tour a gallery of Olivia's old boyfriends, Ken thought grumpily. He walked over to the easel covered by the sheet, planning to lift it for a peek. *It better not be a painting of Rod*

Sullivan! Olivia had dated Rod for a while earlier in the school year.

He lifted the corner of the sheet. When he saw what it was hiding, he pulled the sheet all the way off, letting it fall to the floor. Ken felt as though the wind had been knocked out of him as he gazed at the charcoal drawing on the easel.

That's me, he thought in wonder, his jealousy instantly forgotten. *But it's a me that I didn't know anyone else could see.*

Ken moved closer to the drawing. In the top corner of the easel a small photograph of him was tacked up, which Olivia had taken herself. Olivia was a good photographer, but she'd obviously only used the photograph for reference. Because the difference between the photo and the drawing was as radical as night and day.

He looked OK in the photo, which was a shot of him staring out at the ocean without any real expression on his face. In the drawing, though, Olivia had made Ken look pensive, as if he were thinking about something really deep. *And actually,* Ken thought, as he studied the charcoal drawing, *I look more than a little sad.*

Olivia had added a whole world of understanding to the drawing, as though she'd somehow been able to peer into his very soul. *She saw me for who I really am,* Ken thought in amazement. *She didn't draw me as the captain of the football team or as the regular, easygoing guy everyone else sees.*

Olivia had sketched out a side of him he couldn't have expressed in words, not even if he'd tried for a hundred years.

She knew me so well, Ken realized. His hands began to tremble, and he quickly jammed them into his pockets. *She knew me more intimately than anyone else ever has—and maybe more than anyone else ever will.*

Olivia, he thought, swaying on his feet. *I loved you so much. Why did you have to leave me?*

Ken burst into tears. He didn't even bother to wipe his eyes or to control his emotions. He wept for all he had lost. He'd been given the greatest gift life had to offer—the love of a girl who was full of talent, life, and unspoken understanding—and he'd let her slip through his fingers.

"How can she be gone?" he choked out softly. "Why couldn't I have saved her?"

As Ken lowered his head and covered his face with his hands a calm, soothing voice filled his mind. The voice was low, barely louder than a whisper, but it seemed to echo all through his body, reaching deep down to his core. *There was nothing you could have done,* the voice said, and as Ken listened he swallowed, unable to argue or to deny the truth of those words. *Don't blame yourself.*

Ken didn't know if that voice belonged to a deep part of himself, to a lingering part of Olivia's spirit, or to something else he couldn't understand. But he didn't care. The words cleansed his heart.

But I feel so powerless, he told himself. *So alone. How can I go on without her?*

But Ken realized that he had no other choice. He had to keep living. He had to forgive himself. And he had to go to the memorial service tomorrow and celebrate the life of the girl he had loved with all his heart.

With tears still trailing down his cheeks, Ken headed back downstairs. Mrs. Davidson was waiting for him. She opened her arms as he stepped down into the hallway, and Ken fell into her warm embrace.

"Shhh," Mrs. Davidson whispered as she rocked him gently. "It's all right, honey. It will be all right."

"I'll do it," Ken said softly. "I'll give the eulogy tomorrow."

Mrs. Davidson placed a motherly kiss on his cheek. "I just knew you would," she replied. "I never had a doubt in my mind. Because it's what Olivia would have wanted."

Chapter 12

"Liz! Liz!" Jessica called as she burst through the front door of Fowler Crest. "Liz, come here! Where are you?"

Elizabeth appeared from down the hall. "Jessica? What's going on?"

Still holding the plastic bag filled with Elizabeth's clothing, Jessica ran over and grabbed her twin, lifting her off the ground as she twirled her in the air. "The most amazing thing just happened!" she said. "You'll never believe it!"

"Wow," Elizabeth said as Jessica let her go. "You sure seem to be in a better mood."

"Why wouldn't I be?" Jessica asked. "I just saw a miracle."

"Does it have anything to do with that bag?"

"What? Oh, no," Jessica replied, handing the bag to Elizabeth. "That's just the clothes you left at the hospital. I was there with Marcus—"

"The little boy who's staying with the Santellis?" Elizabeth asked.

"That's him," Jessica said. "I brought him to the hospital to see his father, and I was so worried the whole time. But it turned out great, Liz—Marcus's father is going to be just fine!"

"Oh, Jess, that's so wonderful," Elizabeth replied.

Jessica hugged her twin again. "I can't tell you what a relief it was to see Marcus so happy."

Elizabeth smiled. "I can't tell you what a relief it is to see *you* so happy."

"Where are Mom and Dad?" Jessica demanded. "They've got to hear about this too!"

A frown crossed Elizabeth's face. "Jessica, I need to tell you something—"

At the sight of Elizabeth's expression Jessica's good mood evaporated. "What?" she asked, feeling a sharp twinge of worry.

"You have visitors," Elizabeth replied softly. "In the living room. They're in there with Mom and Dad."

"Who?"

"Now, Jess, I don't want you to freak out—"

"Who's in there?" Jessica asked again, her voice rising.

Elizabeth flinched. "Just try to prepare yourself—"

Jessica couldn't take another second of Elizabeth's nervous waffling. She turned around, strode down the hall, and burst into the elegantly furnished sitting room. Her parents were seated on a long velvet couch, and they looked up as Jessica entered. Mrs. Wakefield offered her a weak smile.

Jessica turned to see who was on the other side of the room, and her stomach clenched.

It was Bryan Hewitt, sitting between two people who could only be his parents.

Jessica suddenly felt weak—all her happiness over seeing Marcus's reunion with his father was completely forgotten.

"Come sit over here by me," Mrs. Wakefield said, patting the space next to her on the couch.

Numbly Jessica nodded and walked over to her mother. "What are they *doing* here?" she hissed.

"I think they should tell you that themselves," Mrs. Wakefield replied.

It took Jessica a full minute to summon enough courage to face the Hewitts.

Mrs. Hewitt's eyes were red rimmed, with dark circles under them. Mr. Hewitt just looked weary and deeply sad.

Between them Bryan sat with his eyes fixed on his hands in his lap, his long dark hair hiding his face.

"Jessica, I'm sorry to surprise you like this," Mrs. Hewitt said. "But Earl and I—" She gestured toward Mr. Hewitt. "We spoke with your parents, and we all agreed that you wouldn't meet with us otherwise. And we all felt this meeting was necessary."

Jessica turned to her parents. "You set this up?" she asked them. "Without telling me?"

"Your mother and I have been very worried about you," Mr. Wakefield said. "We thought it was important to take a drastic step."

"I'm history," Jessica replied, standing up. "See ya."

Mr. Hewitt stood up too. "Please, Jessica," he said. His voice was tinged with so much sorrow that Jessica stopped in her tracks. "Please stay and talk to us. We don't blame you for what happened."

Slowly Jessica turned around to face him. "You don't?" she asked, stunned.

"No, we don't," Mr. Hewitt said. "Please, sit down and talk with us. We won't take up much of your time."

With a deep sigh Jessica returned to her seat beside her mother. Mrs. Wakefield took Jessica's hand in her own, and Jessica gripped it gratefully.

"We never blamed you," Mrs. Hewitt said to Jessica. "When your parents told us how much you were suffering, I just knew we had to see you. I'm sorry we couldn't come sooner, but . . . well, after my daughter . . . when Alyssa . . ." Mrs. Hewitt's voice trailed off, and a tear formed in the corner of her eye. "I'm sorry," she whispered, her voice breaking.

Jessica blinked, trying to will away her own tears.

Mr. Hewitt straightened his jacket. "What my wife is trying to say is that we understand that what happened was an accident," he said somberly. "We don't want you blaming yourself. It was . . . incredibly sad. Alyssa was very special, and there will always be . . . there will always be a hole in my heart where she used to live. There will always be a hole in our family. But it was an *accident*. You must not blame yourself."

"We should *thank* you," Mrs. Hewitt managed to choke out.

Jessica sat up straight on the couch and let go of her mother's hand. "*Thank* me?" she asked. She swallowed, clearing a lump in her throat. "Why would you thank me?"

"For trying so hard to save our daughter," Mr. Hewitt replied. "You didn't even know her. You didn't have to stop to help on the road that day. Alyssa was a complete stranger to you. That's why we should thank you."

Jessica was at a loss for words. *But I didn't try hard enough,* she replied silently. *I should have done more. I should have been able to save her!*

Mrs. Hewitt wiped her eyes with a tissue. "All I can say is, your parents did a wonderful job of raising you, Jessica. To try so hard to help a stranger . . . You were raised *right*. It's good to know there are still people like you in the world. I'd want Alyssa to learn from you if she hadn't . . ." Mrs. Hewitt starting sobbing quietly again.

Jessica ducked her head as she struggled to keep from crying. The Hewitts were impossibly sweet, going out of their way to reassure her that their daughter's death wasn't her fault. If only she could believe them!

"Bryan has something to say to you too," Mr.

Hewitt told Jessica. He nudged his son's arm. "Don't you, Bryan?"

"No," Bryan replied sullenly. He didn't lift his head.

"Bryan!" Mrs. Hewitt scolded. "We discussed this in the car."

Bryan just crossed his arms over his chest.

"He doesn't have to say anything," Jessica said. "It's OK, really."

"Don't force the boy," Mr. Wakefield added. "He's been through a terrible shock. We all need our own pace to mourn—"

"Don't talk about me like I'm not here!" Bryan shouted. "I was there! I watched it happen!" He pointed at Jessica with a shaking finger. "And it was all her fault!"

Tears started to stream down Jessica's face as she choked out a sob. "I know," she cried. "I *know.*"

"Bryan!" Mrs. Hewitt protested. "Tell Jessica you're sorry. Tell her you didn't mean it!"

"No way," Brian spat out. "She killed my little sister. She *deserves* to blame herself."

Jessica jumped to her feet. "He's right," she sobbed, weaving slightly as she stumbled toward the door. "It was all my fault!"

Blinded by her own tears, Jessica fled the room.

Elizabeth sat down on her temporary bed and opened the bag of clothing Jessica had brought her from the hospital. A weird smell hit her nose as soon as she opened it, but Elizabeth couldn't immediately identify the scent. It was a chemical smell, mixed with the odor of burned fabric. . . .

Shaking her head, Elizabeth reached in and pulled out a pair of black jeans and a cute fuchsia blouse—the outfit she'd been wearing at her seventeenth birthday party, when the earthquake had struck.

I was so excited when I put these on, Elizabeth recalled. *When I was getting ready to throw Jessica a surprise party at the Beach Disco.*

But the Beach Disco party hadn't worked out, and she'd been miserable—and afraid of her twin's reaction to the canceled event—when she returned home. Then everything had seemed great again when she found out that all her and Jessica's friends had gotten together to throw them a joint surprise birthday party in the Wakefields' backyard. She'd been having an excellent time too, until . . .

Until the celebration ended in tragedy, Elizabeth remembered. But that's *all* she could remember. Everything from the moment the ground had begun to shake was still a complete blank.

Elizabeth brought the blouse up to her face and sniffed it, trying again to place the odd scent that was filling the room. *That's funny,* she thought. *It almost smells like . . . like chlorine.*

Was I in the pool? she wondered. *Did I fall in? Was that the water I mentioned to Maria when I was under hypnosis?*

It couldn't be. Devon would have definitely

mentioned it if she'd fallen into the pool sometime during the evening. There had to be some other explanation.

Elizabeth checked the ankles of the jeans and, as she suspected, they had burn marks on them.

How had she gotten burned? Devon had mentioned nothing about her being close to the fire that had swept into the Wakefields' backyard.

Oh, it's all just so confusing, she thought, stuffing the clothing back into the bag. *And incredibly frustrating!*

If only she could remember, she could lay the whole awful mystery to rest. Elizabeth flopped back on the bed, squeezing her eyes shut. She willed herself to remember. *Think, Liz, think,* she ordered herself. *Those memories are in there somewhere!*

But after a few moments of recalling absolutely nothing, Elizabeth gave up. *All I know is that I've dreamed about eels, worried about how heavy Enid was, screamed to Devon, and somehow got all wet with pool water,* she thought, trying to piece it all together. *Oh, and something about a snake . . .*

But no matter how she turned her few memories over in her mind, they refused to paint a complete picture of what had happened.

Maybe Devon wasn't *telling the whole truth,* Elizabeth thought. *There do seem to be a few holes in his story. Maybe Maria was right after all. . . .*

No. She had to believe Devon had told her

everything that had occurred. Because what would that mean about him if he hadn't?

With a sigh, Elizabeth stood up and headed toward the bathroom to wash the smell of chlorine off her hands.

From her bed Jessica stared out the window at the Fowlers' magnificently landscaped backyard. She could just make out the edge of the tennis courts on one end of the lawn and nearby, the cute little gazebo peeking out of a stand of trees. Jessica's window was directly over the back patio, which was a large rectangle of red clay tiles, decorated with hanging baskets of plants and surrounded by lemon trees.

Jessica sighed miserably. Looking at the beautiful view gave her absolutely no pleasure. Bryan had just confirmed all the darkest thoughts she'd had, and she couldn't help wondering if it had been a mistake to have stopped what she was about to do to herself at Secca Lake. *Maybe the world would be better off without me,* she thought. *Even Marcus won't miss me, now that he's back with his father.* Her eyes were dry. Jessica had no more tears left.

Jessica's bleak thoughts were interrupted by a knock at the door. "Go away!" she shouted without looking away from the view outside her window. There was nobody she wanted to talk to. Nobody at all.

Behind her Jessica heard the door open.

Irritated, she turned around. "I said, *go away*," she spat out. "Are you deaf?"

Bryan stood in the doorway, glaring at her. The expression on his face was both miserable and angry. "Believe me, I'd love to," he replied. "I'd rather be anyplace else. But my parents won't let me leave without talking to you."

"You don't have to tell me again that it was my fault," Jessica said coldly. "I know, and I'm sorry. But nothing I can do can change what happened."

"Just don't talk to me," Bryan replied. He leaned against the wall by the door and crossed his arms. "Let's just not say anything, and in a little while I'll go back down and tell my parents we're cool. OK?"

"Sure," Jessica said. "No problem. Silence it is."

Bryan looked down at his feet as Jessica sat on the bed, waiting for the moment when he decided he'd been up here long enough for him to leave.

But Jessica had never been good at sitting quietly.

"I know you can never forgive me for what happened," she told Bryan. "But I can't forgive myself either."

Bryan narrowed his eyes. "Is that supposed to make me feel better?" he asked. "My little sister is *dead*."

"No," Jessica replied, flinching at the tone of his words. "It's not supposed to make you feel better. Nothing can do that, I know. I'm just trying to explain, that's all."

"Well, don't," Bryan shot back. He pushed his messy brown hair off his forehead. "Just shut up, OK? I don't want to hear anything you have to say."

Jessica let her legs slide off the edge of the bed. "Why are you being so horrible?" she asked in a hurt voice. "I didn't do it on purpose. You've got to understand that—"

"Just shut up!" Bryan yelled at her, his face turning red. "I don't have to understand anything! Why did you even stop your Jeep if you couldn't help?" He rubbed his hand over his forehead, his voice lowering to a pathetic whisper. "Why couldn't you save her?"

How many times had Jessica asked herself the same question? How many nights had she lain awake, wondering what else she could have tried to save Alyssa? She'd failed, and she knew that. But it was one thing for her to accuse herself, and it was quite another for Bryan to stand there and try to lay all the blame on her. "Hey, you were there too!" she told him bitterly, pressing her palms down on the mattress.

Bryan started to cry and let himself slide down the wall until he was sitting on the floor. "I know," he said weakly. "I know."

Surprised by his reaction, Jessica crossed her arms and stared at him. "What . . . ," she asked him, "what are you talking about?"

"It was all me," Bryan replied.

"No," Jessica said. "It was my fault. That's already been decided."

Bryan shook his head. "You're wrong," he told her. "I was wrong."

"Then why did you say it was my fault? Do you know how awful that made me feel? Not that it's something I wasn't thinking myself, of course—"

"Don't say that," Bryan broke in, looking up at her earnestly with his damp brown eyes. "I'm sorry I said you . . . killed Alyssa. I shouldn't have said that. That . . . that wasn't right of me to say. I'm so sorry, really."

"Why did you say it, then?" Jessica asked.

Bryan was silent a moment as he looked down at his hands. "I guess I was just blaming you . . . because it was too painful to blame myself."

Jessica couldn't find any words to reply. She just stared at Bryan as she began to tremble—from shock or sadness or exhaustion, she couldn't tell which.

"I'm so sorry I was horrible to you," Bryan mumbled. "I don't blame you, really. It wasn't your fault at all. It was mine."

Jessica slid off the bed and took a few steps toward Bryan. "Come here," she said.

Bryan looked up at her, surprised, as she stood over him. When she opened her arms, he quickly climbed to his feet and fell into her hug. Jessica held him as he shook with deep sobs.

"I'm so sorry, Jessica," he cried. "Can you ever forgive me?"

"Only if you promise to forgive yourself," Jessica replied. She ran her hand gently over the back of his head, soothing him. "It wasn't your fault either, and you have to believe that. Bryan, please try to believe that. If you don't, you're only going to hurt yourself. I know."

Jessica held him tight as he nodded against her shoulder. "I'll try," he promised, and he broke into a fresh wave of sobs.

Resting her head against his, Jessica let out a long breath of air—a breath she felt she'd been holding ever since the earthquake. For the first time in a long time, she wasn't the one crying.

"It wasn't either of our faults," Jessica whispered. "It was an earthquake."

Chapter 13

"Please, everyone, take a seat," Mrs. Davidson told the crowd gathered in her small backyard on Wednesday morning.

Elizabeth sat down in a folding chair between Enid and Maria Slater. She quickly took one of each of her best friends' hands in her own, holding on tightly. Elizabeth was going to need all the support she could get to make it through Olivia's memorial service, especially since just the sight of the crowd of Olivia's friends who had come to say good-bye made Elizabeth want to burst into miserable tears.

"Pull it together, Wakefield," Maria whispered into her ear. "It hasn't even started yet."

"Here," Enid said, offering Elizabeth a tissue. "I brought extra."

"Thanks," Elizabeth replied with a sniffle. "You guys are the best."

Mr. Davidson walked up to the white podium that had been set up in front of the rows of folding chairs. The podium was decorated with palm fronds and silver draperies, with small apricot flowers attached. Elizabeth thought it looked quite lovely—elegant, but still appropriate for the funky girl they'd all come to remember.

"Thank you all for coming," Mr. Davidson said as he took his wife's hand. "We've reserved today to give everyone an opportunity to remember Olivia, my daughter—to share with everyone present all the little ways she touched our lives. Tomorrow morning we're going to go down to the beach to scatter my daughter's ashes in the ocean, and you're all welcome to join us there as well."

"Please, anyone who wishes to say something about Olivia, just stand up and speak," Mrs. Davidson said. "Ken Matthews has been kind enough to agree to give a more formal eulogy in a few minutes, but this time is for you."

After a moment of uncomfortable silence in the crowd, Penny Ayala stood up. Penny was a good friend of Elizabeth's, and the lanky brunette was also editor in chief of the *Oracle*. "I've considered Olivia a friend nearly from the first day she showed up in the *Oracle* office with a folder full of photographs," Penny said, her voice low and serious. "One look at her, and you could just see she was an artist. It took me only a few weeks to appoint her as arts editor of the newspaper. . . . I had simply never met anyone else nearly as qualified for the job." Penny paused a moment and then muttered, "I promised myself I wouldn't talk about the newspaper." A polite laugh rippled through the crowd, and Penny smiled shyly, encouraged by the audience's support. "She was my friend," Penny said, her voice breaking. "And I don't have many people I consider true friends. I loved her very much, and I'm so sorry she's gone. Olivia, I will miss you."

Penny sat down again and hugged her boyfriend, Neil Freemount. Elizabeth wiped her eyes as Roger Barrett Patman climbed to his feet.

Roger's face was slack, and his gray eyes were filled with tears. The tall track star had dated Olivia for a long time, although their breakup had been mutual and peaceful. "Olivia was the sweetest girl I've ever known," Roger told the crowd. "She helped me so much during one of the worst times in my life—when my mother died—but even after we broke up, she was always there for me if I needed her. I can't even begin to say how much I'll miss her. I don't . . . know what else to say except that I miss her so much."

Rod Sullivan stood up near Roger. "You know Olivia was amazing if I dated her and we broke up and I *still* like all her other boyfriends," he said. The audience laughed, and Rod smiled. "I'm glad to hear all of you laugh. Because that was a big part of what Olivia stood for—having fun. She could be incredibly passionate about her art and deadly serious about it too, but never let anyone tell you that

185

Olivia didn't know how to cut loose. That's what I'll always remember about her, that she could be so wild and free."

Elizabeth nodded and wiped away a tear as Rod sat down. Before she could even think about what she was doing, Elizabeth stood up herself. "Hi," she said, blood rushing to her face as everyone turned to look at her. "Uh . . . like Penny, I considered Olivia one of my best friends," she said. "She was always ready to listen whenever I needed her, and she would help me lighten up when I got too down on myself or confused. She was an amazing artist too, and she made working on the newspaper so much fun." Elizabeth stopped speaking for a moment, aware that she wasn't getting to the heart of what she wanted to say. "Olivia was unique," she finally said simply. "There was nobody else like her, and there never will be. All I know is that I will miss her so very much."

With a sob Elizabeth collapsed back in her chair. Enid reached over and put her arm around Elizabeth's shoulders. She let herself cry. *I didn't say enough,* she thought worriedly. *But maybe there was no way to really express the depth of the loss I feel.*

As Elizabeth wiped her eyes she saw that Devon had stood up after her. "I didn't know Olivia very long," Devon said somberly, "but what I did know of her impressed me greatly. . . ."

Elizabeth was suddenly distracted by Dana Larson shifting in the chair in front of her. Dana struggled to remove her jacket—she was probably getting hot in the bright sun. As Dana settled down again Elizabeth glanced at her . . . and gasped as her gaze fell on the silver arm cuff Dana was wearing.

The arm cuff was in the shape of a hissing snake.

The snake, Elizabeth thought as her stomach dropped. *How could I have forgotten the rattlesnake in the pool?*

Suddenly, like a dam had burst open within her, all Elizabeth's lost memories came flooding back in a huge, horrifying wave. For a long, dizzying moment she felt as if she were about to faint.

But then her head stopped swimming and quickly cleared. The eels in her dreams didn't just represent the power lines like she'd originally thought—she'd totally forgotten about the poisonous snake that had hissed threateningly at her in the swimming pool!

And I had to pull myself out of the pool, Elizabeth remembered, her eyes growing wide. *Because Devon had totally abandoned me!*

Elizabeth's mouth fell open, and she felt completely nauseated. *That was when I scraped my knees—on the concrete around the pool,* she recalled. *And then I . . . I pulled Enid away from the fire myself!*

She remembered everything now—all the pain and horror and panic of that evening after the earthquake. The fire had burned her ankles as she ran through a ring of flames to reach Enid. Devon had fled, ignoring her screams for help.

Elizabeth still didn't know who had pulled her away from the power lines after she'd been shocked herself, but now she knew with absolute certainty that it wasn't Devon. *That boy was so scared,* she remembered. *There was no way he turned around again to help me!*

And Devon had accepted the credit for rescuing her.

Elizabeth covered her mouth with her hand as she considered the enormity of what he had done. *How could he . . . ?* she wondered in shock. *I can't even believe it!*

But now that she had her memories back, Elizabeth knew that it was true. The shock was so overwhelming, she nearly forgot she was at a memorial service. She had to fight to stay composed. Devon had left her to die in her backyard . . . and then he had accepted her *thanks* for being her hero. It was the most awful thing anyone had ever done to her. It was the most awful thing she'd ever even heard of!

I wanted to kiss *him,* Elizabeth thought in disbelief. *I was jealous of Enid!*

That . . . that maggot! That unbelievable, worthless slime!

"Without her talent we never would have won the Battle of the Junior Classes," Devon was saying as Elizabeth returned her attention to him. "I just wanted everyone here to know how much I was impressed by her creativity. Thank you."

As he turned to sit down Elizabeth caught his eye, knowing all the confusion, anger, and complete horror she felt was reflected in her face. Devon flinched.

He knows that I know, Elizabeth realized.

She kept him pinned in her gaze as his expression shifted from scared to guilty. He kept his shoulders stiff as he turned around and looked away from her.

The hero has fallen back to earth, Elizabeth thought as rage built up within her. If only she'd remembered sooner. All Elizabeth wanted to do was scream at Devon and demand to know why he'd lied—and why he'd left her to die. Unfortunately this wasn't the time for that.

But it was no matter. Very soon now Devon Whitelaw would get exactly what he deserved.

In the front row of the crowd Ken sat in a state of shock as he listened to everyone praise Olivia. He'd known his girlfriend was popular, but there was no way he could have prepared himself for the depth of emotion her friends were expressing as they spoke about her short life.

Nicholas Morrow stood up. Ken didn't know the dark-haired, mysterious guy very well, but Nicholas was the kind of guy any girl fell for. Ken

189

knew that Nicholas was considered to be extraordinarily handsome, and he spent most of his time sailing up and down the coast of California on his enormous yacht. Nicholas was very wealthy and had always struck Ken as the kind of guy who always knew what to do.

"Many of you here know I lost my sister, Regina," Nicholas was saying in his deep voice, his piercing emerald eyes glistening with moisture.

Ken nodded sadly. It was common knowledge that beautiful, sweet Regina had died from a bad reaction to cocaine—the first time she'd tried the dangerous drug. Everyone at Sweet Valley High had mourned Regina for a very long time.

"Olivia was a good friend to me during that difficult point in my life," Nicholas continued. "She didn't hurry me to get over Regina's death and supported me when I was feeling too sad to go on. For that I will always be grateful to her, more than I can ever say."

Nicholas swallowed and fell silent for a moment as he struggled with his emotions. "I never told Olivia this," he said softly, "and now I'm sorry that I never did. But I thought of her as a sister. I don't know what I'm going to do without her. Olivia, if you can hear me, I'm sorry I never told you how much I loved you. And I hope you will always think of me, wherever you are, as your loving brother down here on earth. Say hello to Regina for me."

Ken sniffled and took a deep breath as Nicholas

sat down. How much love his girlfriend had spread through life, how many hearts she had touched! Ken's eyes grew hot and sore as he forced himself not to cry. He'd promised himself that he would get through his eulogy without garbling it with tears, and once he'd started crying, he was sure he wouldn't be able to stop. For Olivia's sake he would make sure everyone heard every word.

Mrs. Davidson approached the podium again, dabbing at her eyes with a handkerchief. "Thank you all for your lovely sentiments," she told the crowd. "I've found them all so truly touching." She closed her eyes for a moment until she could speak in a steady voice again. "Now I'd like to welcome Ken Matthews up to the podium to give the more formal eulogy he's planned for us. Ken?"

Shaking with nerves, Ken rose and walked up to the podium. "Thanks," he said. His voice came out in a croak. "I'm just a dumb football jock and not nearly as creative . . . or as good at . . . expressing myself as Olivia was, so I wrote down what I wanted to say."

He quickly pulled a sheet of paper out of his back pocket, and his hands shook as he spread it out on the podium. For a few seconds Ken stood still, taking deep breaths, trying to calm himself. Then in a loud, steady voice he began to read.

"I first met Olivia Davidson way back when we were kids," Ken read. "But I didn't really *know* her until a few months ago. That was when I met

Freeverse on the Internet, in a chat room.

"I had no idea that Freeverse was Olivia," Ken continued. "Neither of us knew the other's true identity. My screen name was Quarter, and that's how we talked for a long time, as Freeverse and Quarter. And we had the most amazing on-line conversations. We would pretend we were taking long walks on the beach, and Freeverse was so good at describing the surroundings she imagined. I could picture myself there along with her—I could smell the ocean as long as she was describing it. But best of all, she taught me how to describe things too, and I've never felt my imagination working like it did when I was chatting with her.

"It was like she brought me deeper into myself," Ken read. "She saw a side of me nobody had ever seen before. Freeverse was the first person who ever inspired my imagination, and I fell in love with her before I ever met her face-to-face. By meeting the way we did, we somehow managed to look behind our masks, you know? The masks that everybody has up all the time. Freeverse was an amazing person, and I was pretty sure I would love her no matter what she looked like . . . although I knew she had to be beautiful. And of course she was."

Ken pushed his blond hair off his forehead and took a deep breath before returning to his speech. "At first I think Olivia was put off by who I turned out to be. Like I had pretended to be this guy who could really talk to her—this guy who understood her imagination. I think she thought I'd been making fun of her or something. But that was so not true. It took a little while, but eventually I managed to explain that she'd brought out something new in me, something I treasured. And eventually she believed I loved her.

"The days I spent with her were the best in my life. Once she saw that the Quarter she loved really was inside me, she worked hard to keep inspiring my soul . . . which she did every single day."

Ken licked his lips, fighting down the sorrow and loneliness that was aching in his heart. "That's what was so incredible about her," he read. "She could see the best thing about everybody she met. She could look deeper, into your heart, and talk to that place where you were your best self possible. She always had a smile for everybody and made everyone feel inspired."

He couldn't struggle against his tears much longer. "The world is a worse place without her," Ken read, his voice breaking. "But it will never be a terrible place because of all the love she shared when she was here."

Tears started to run down his face, but Ken paid them no mind. He was almost done, and it seemed right to cry for Olivia, for all the love he had lost. "I will miss her always," he sobbed out. "But I'm glad I got to love her."

Openly weeping, Ken stumbled back to his seat. As soon as he sat down he covered his face with his hands, letting himself cry out all his awful, lonely sadness. He felt his mother beside him, rubbing his back with her hand, but Ken stayed where he was, allowing his tears to express the sorrow in his heart.

He knew he would feel the pain of her absence forever, but it was so important that he'd had the chance to say good-bye.

Tears trickled down Lila's cheeks.

Beside her Amy Sutton turned to her in alarm. "Lila," she asked softly, "are you OK?"

"I'm fine," Lila whispered. That wasn't true, but Amy didn't need to know much more than that. "Ken's speech was just so moving, you know?"

"Totally," Amy agreed. "It was amazingly sad."

Lila nodded and noticed that the seat on her other side was empty. "Do you know where Jessica went?" she asked Amy.

"Um . . . ," Amy replied. "I think she went to look for Liz. I'm not sure, though. Maybe she just didn't want to listen to Ken. Things haven't been that great between them since she cheated on him."

"Amy!" Lila chided. "This is not the time or the place for gossip."

"Well, it's true," Amy said.

"I guess so," Lila replied. "But it didn't seem very appropriate to say."

"Whatever," Amy countered. "I'm going to look for Jessica. You want to come?"

"No," Lila answered. "I think I'll stay here for a little while."

"Suit yourself," Amy chirped, and then she was off.

Lila hugged herself, crunching the strange fabric of the black John Galliano dress she was wearing, wondering why she had snapped at Amy for her little remark. It was the kind of thing they said to each other all the time, just another morsel of tasty gossip to share. So why had she re-acted with such irritation?

Guilt, Lila answered herself. All during Ken's eulogy she'd been attacking herself for being so shallow and snobby. Ken's words about how deep Olivia was had really hit home.

I always thought Olivia was too weird to be friends with, she realized. *I never gave her a chance!*

The way Ken had spoken about Olivia, she'd sounded like a lovely girl, open and honest and nonjudgmental—everything that Lila was not.

I'll never let my snobbery get in the way ever again, Lila vowed. *Life is too short.*

Again hot tears poured from Lila's eyes. *Because I was a snob,* Lila thought, *I lost the chance to know somebody really valuable. Somebody who could have known the real me!* Somebody who could have looked behind the rich, reserved, chilly mask Lila al-ways wore and could have seen the frightened little girl hiding inside.

I could have had a real friend, Lila realized.

Lila covered her eyes with her arm. *I'm the worst person who ever lived!* she thought miserably. *And I don't deserve to have any friends at all!*

Just then Lila felt strong arms embracing her. She recognized the warm, masculine scent. "Todd," she whispered. "Oh, Todd."

"Hi," he said softly. "Are you all right?"

"No," Lila replied, her eyes swimming with tears as she heard the genuine concern in his voice. "No, I'm not."

Then she sank her head against his chest and wept.

Chapter 14

Elizabeth stood on her tiptoes, scanning the crowd for any sign of Devon. She needed to get him alone—away from Olivia's parents and the rest of the mourners—and confront him. He couldn't get away with his deceit any longer. *If he's managed to escape without hearing what I have to say to him, I'll be so furious!* she thought hotly.

But then Elizabeth spotted him sneaking through the crowd, heading for the gate that led out of the Davidsons' backyard. Elizabeth narrowed her eyes and hurried toward him, determined to head him off before he could run away.

She caught up with him just outside the gate. Before he could say anything, she grabbed his arm and pulled him to the end of the driveway. She stopped beneath a palm tree at the edge of the Davidsons' property and turned to face him.

Everyone else was still milling around the back-yard, so Elizabeth and Devon were completely alone. "Devon," she said, "we need to talk."

"Not right now, Liz," he said brusquely.

"You're going to listen to me," Elizabeth shot back. "Did you lie to me about rescuing me and Enid?"

"Liz," Devon said with a sigh, "what are you *talking* about?"

"I think you know!" Elizabeth told him. His feigning infuriated her. "And let me tell you, Devon Whitelaw, what you did is absolutely *disgusting!* How could you take credit for saving us when you knew you hadn't? It's just . . . unbelievable!"

"Then don't believe it," Devon replied calmly. "Who told you this anyway?"

"Nobody," Elizabeth said. "I figured it out on my own. How could you do this to me, Devon? I *trusted* you. I even argued on your behalf! And now I find that you've been completely *lying* to me the whole time? Do you know how awful that is?" Elizabeth's eyes filled with tears. She hated that she was doing this. She was supposed to be re-membering Olivia with her friends, and instead she was trying to drag the truth out of a worthless liar. But she had to know what happened and why Devon had left her.

"I thought you couldn't remember," Devon protested.

"My memories came back," Elizabeth informed him, a single tear spilling over. "How could you just leave me and Enid there? We could have *died!*"

"Do you remember everything?" Devon asked.

Elizabeth wiped her cheek, not knowing how to reply. She definitely didn't want to give him any ammunition to weasel out of what he'd done. But she couldn't lie to him as awfully as he'd lied to her. There was no way she was going to sink down to his level. "No," she admitted, "I still don't know who pulled me away from the wires. But I'm sure it wasn't you!"

"How do you know?" Devon asked. His sudden icy smugness made Elizabeth almost want to slap him. "You said yourself that you don't know who it was."

Elizabeth's tears cleared and she glared at him, feeling betrayed worse than she'd ever been in her life. Even when directly confronted with the truth, Devon still wouldn't come clean. She couldn't believe she'd been in love with someone so deceitful. For him she'd turned her whole life upside down! For him she'd even thrown away Todd. Now that he'd tricked her, Elizabeth couldn't believe the mess she'd made of her life in the name of love. How had she managed to be such a total fool?

Todd rocked gently with Lila in his arms. Comforting her felt so good—almost as good as she herself felt against him. He let her cry, holding her tightly so she'd feel secure in his embrace. As he leaned down to get closer to her he caught a hint of her wonderful, complicated perfume. It made him feel a little dizzy and tender toward her at the same time.

Why did I wait so long to hold her in my arms? Todd wondered. He reached out and stroked her long brown hair, which felt impossibly soft under his fingertips, just as he'd known it would.

"Shhh," he whispered as her sobs began tapering off.

"It's just so sad," she said miserably.

"It's all right," he crooned to her. Todd wondered for the thousandth time what it would be like to kiss her. There were so many feelings and thoughts whirling around in his mind. He felt as if everything were ending—Olivia was gone, the school year was over, his relationship with Elizabeth. . . . All he wanted at that moment was to feel hope. To feel as if everything good in life hadn't just gone up in smoke. Before he could stop himself, he leaned over and kissed Lila softly on the lips.

Lila stiffened in Todd's arms. And Todd felt . . . nothing.

Slowly pulling away, Lila straightened her skirt and cleared her throat, averting her eyes.

"What was that?" she asked with an embarrassed laugh.

"That was . . ." How could Todd answer that? He'd thought she'd wanted him to kiss her. And he'd thought . . . no, *known* it was going to be electric.

But it wasn't. In fact, it was the most blah kiss he'd ever experienced. "Sorry," he said finally. "Guess I just got carried away."

Lila's face reddened and she jumped out of her chair, grabbing her small black purse. "I cannot believe you just kissed me! At a *funeral!*" Lila hissed through her teeth. "What kind of tactless jerk are you?"

Todd stared at her. "Lila, calm down." He glanced around, but so far no one seemed to have noticed her outburst. "You're making a scene."

"I'm making a scene?" Lila shouted. "I can't believe I ever thought of *changing* myself because of you. I can't believe I ever—"

"Changing yourself for me?" Todd said. He laughed, unable to believe he'd ever felt any kind of tenderness toward the biggest snob in the history of Sweet Valley. "Are you kidding? You'd have to get conked on the head and wake up with a new personality before I'd glance your way."

Lila's eyes were on fire, and Todd realized that if this little argument didn't end soon, they were risking destroying a perfectly sentimental service. "Lila, I—"

"Save it, Wilkins," Lila whispered, leaning in close. "I'm outta here, but let me just tell you one thing first." Her eyes narrowed, and for a moment Todd felt like a caged rabbit. "You're the worst kisser I've ever had the displeasure of meeting lips with." She stood up straight. "No wonder Elizabeth dumped you. It was the smartest thing that dork ever did." With that Lila stuck her nose in the air and stalked away.

Todd took a deep breath and leaned back in his chair. He'd thought he'd glimpsed a vulnerable side to Lila Fowler, but after that little display it was obvious the girl was as heartless as ever. Todd just hoped Elizabeth hadn't seen them kiss.

Sliding down low in his chair, Todd cast a look around. Elizabeth was nowhere to be found.

Thank God, Todd thought. If Elizabeth had seen him kiss Lila Fowler, he'd be paying for that moment of weakness for the rest of his life. Elizabeth would never speak to him again. Even though he was still angry at Elizabeth over Devon, that kiss with Lila had proved to him that there was only one girl in his heart. Maybe they'd agreed to take a break from each other for now, but Todd wasn't ready to let her go for good.

Not by a long shot.

Lila stalked across the Davidsons' tiny backyard, her expensive black heels sinking into the soft ground. *I have never been so disgusted in my entire life,* she silently fumed. How could she have ever let her guard down? How could she have admitted to Todd that she'd thought of changing for him?

As Lila pushed through the side gate she heard Amy calling out her name. Lila stopped and whirled around, not bothering to mask her irritation.

"What is it, Amy?" she snapped.

"Chill! Lila, have you completely lost it? Did I just see you *kiss* Todd Wilkins?" Amy asked, her eyes wide.

Lila took a deep breath and let it out slowly through her nose. She would have to handle this situation very carefully. Amy was the second-biggest gossip in school—next to Caroline Pearce. "First of all, *he* kissed *me,* not the other way around," Lila began. "Second, it was the worst kiss I've ever experienced." Lila leaned in closer to Amy, leveling her with a glare. "And if you ever tell anyone about this, you will be very sorry."

Amy smirked. "Oh, really, Lila?" she said. "And what exactly are you going to do to me?"

Lila blinked. She had absolutely no idea what she would do to Amy. What was happening to her? Where were her quick comebacks? Her snide remarks? Her patented quiver-inducing threats?

"I have an idea," Amy said, throwing an arm around Lila's shoulders. "Maybe we can make a deal."

Amy started to steer Lila toward her car. A deal. This was more like it. "Interesting," Lila said. "What kind of deal are we talking about here?"

"Oh, the kind where you take me shopping for school clothes in the fall and charge them to your father along with yours," Amy answered with a grin.

Lila felt a mischievous grin spread across her face. "But Amy, darling, Daddy would get suspicious when he got the statements. He knows I would never stoop to shop at those flea markets you call boutiques."

Amy's face fell, but she recovered as she slid into the passenger seat of the Triumph. "Well, then, Ms. Fashion Plate, why don't we go shopping right now and you can teach me all your incredible secrets of style?"

"Sounds like a plan," Lila said. Running up some credit card bills would be just the thing to take her mind off that loser Todd and all the sappy dorks at the funeral. She didn't need them. Lila Fowler could take care of herself.

She revved the engine, cranked the radio, and peeled out into the street, leaving all thoughts of Olivia, Todd, and the "new and improved Lila" behind.

"I'm giving you one last chance to tell me the truth," Elizabeth told Devon. "I know I was the one who pulled Enid out of that fire in my back-yard—I even have the burned socks to prove it. But I want to hear it from your own lips. Just tell me that you didn't rescue me, and I'll let you go."

"Nope," Devon replied, sounding sullen and bitter. He didn't look up at her and began stubbing out a small dandelion on the lawn with his toe. "Maybe I wasn't there to pull Enid out of the fire," he said, "but I came back to pull you two out of range of the power lines."

Elizabeth gasped. "That's so not true!" she told him, feeling fury mounting inside her. "I begged you to come help me save Enid. And you refused over and over again!"

"I came back," Devon said stubbornly.

"Stop lying!" Elizabeth shouted. "I saw you running for your life with my own eyes! There's no way you would have come back—you were too scared. There's just no way!"

"You don't know that," Devon said.

"Will you stop *lying* to me?" Elizabeth yelled. "Please!"

Her angry words were starting to draw the attention of the other mourners filtering out of the backyard.

"We're going to have company in a minute," Elizabeth informed Devon. "Do you want to tell me what really happened privately, or do you want the whole world to know?"

Devon glanced up, and he pressed his lips together as he saw Ken, Jessica, Enid, Maria Slater, and a few others heading their way. "I already told you what happened," he hissed at Elizabeth, sounding desperate.

"Is everything all right, Lizzie?" Jessica asked when she reached them.

"No, Jess, it's not all right," Elizabeth said, her emotions too strong to hold inside. "I finally got all my memories back, and I remembered that Devon deserted me and Enid. All this time he's been taking the credit for rescuing me, but he really just left me there to die." Elizabeth dissolved into tears, and Jessica held her in stunned silence.

"I don't believe this," Enid said, her eyes wide.

"Devon's been taking credit for saving you?" Ken asked.

"This is none of your business, Ken," Devon said. "Please let us handle this on our own."

"I'm making it my business," Ken replied, a scowl crossing his handsome, weary features. "Because I happen to know you didn't rescue Elizabeth or Enid."

"What?" Elizabeth gasped. "How do you know?"

"I'm sorry I didn't say anything to you before," Ken apologized to Elizabeth. "But I didn't realize Devon had lied. I've been kind of wrapped up in . . . other things lately."

"That's OK," Elizabeth assured her friend quickly. "Just tell me how you know."

"That's it," Devon said. "I'm out of here." He tried to push past Elizabeth, but Ken grabbed the back of his jacket and stopped him. "Get your hands off me!" Devon shouted at Ken.

"Hey, relax, buddy. I don't want to make a scene here," Ken said, smoothing down the front of Devon's jacket. "If you saved the girls, then there's no reason to run, right? So why don't you stay and listen to what I have to say?"

"Good point," Maria added.

"Yeah," Jessica said. "What's the big hurry, Devon?"

Elizabeth's heart swelled with pride at the way

her friends were standing up for her—and she especially felt proud of Ken. Even as hard hit as he obviously was about Olivia's death, he was still taking the time to help her out. *He's a great friend,* Elizabeth thought. *No wonder I had that crush on him for a while.* The struggle between Ken and Devon settled down, and Devon stood uncomfortably a few feet away from Elizabeth. He stuck his hands into the pockets of his jacket and stared down at the driveway.

"OK," Ken said. "Here's what I saw. When I was rushing back to Olivia with the EMTs, I happened to look over to the other end of the backyard—to check the progress of the fire, I guess. But I also saw this stranger pulling Elizabeth away from the power lines. Enid was already in a safe area."

A stranger? Elizabeth wondered, her eyes wide. "Who was it?" she asked.

"I have no idea," Ken replied. "And I was too freaked out to check, you know? But I know for sure it wasn't Whitelaw here. He was nowhere to be seen."

"That fits with what I heard," Maria put in. "I already told Liz that I heard her arguing with Devon—and him refusing to help."

"I'm so sorry I didn't believe you," Elizabeth told her. "I should have trusted you all along."

"No problem," Maria said with a smile. "Just as long as this creep gets what's coming to him."

"Oh, he will," Elizabeth replied, turning to face Devon.

Slowly Devon raised his head. His brilliant gray-blue eyes were blazing with anger, pain . . . and fear. He looked like a wounded animal with its paw caught in a trap.

But Elizabeth refused to let his powerful emotions affect her. She was far too mad at him for that.

"So?" she demanded to know. "You heard them. What do you think of all *that*?"

Panic made Devon's heart flutter like a scared bird's. Elizabeth and the others were staring at him, waiting for his reply. But he had run out of things to say.

Devon closed his eyes for a moment, feeling exhausted, guilty, and ashamed of himself. *If I tell them the truth, I'll never have any friends in Sweet Valley again,* he realized. *Why didn't I just tell the truth from the beginning?*

That question was easy to answer. He'd lied because he loved Elizabeth, and he had wanted her to look at him with love in her eyes. He'd lied because he couldn't stand the thought of her hating him . . . the way she did now.

The real question was a lot harder for him to deal with.

Why did I abandon Elizabeth after the earthquake?

That was the question that had kept him up at night.

"Well?" Elizabeth asked, her voice sharp with anger. "Devon, we're waiting. . . ."

Devon looked at her, ready to spill another lie. He could say he'd helped the stranger at the last minute. He could say that yes, he'd run away, but that he'd felt bad about it and had come back. Maybe he could even get everyone to believe him.

But then Devon shook his head. *No more lies,* he told himself. *There's no way out.*

"Yes," he told Elizabeth miserably. "Yes, you're all right. Is that what you wanted to hear?"

"So you admit the truth?" Elizabeth asked, sounding a little shocked at his revelation . . . almost as though she had still held a tiny torch of hope that he hadn't abandoned her.

How he hated to squelch that hope! But he'd said too much to stop now. "I ran away," Devon replied flatly. "I left you there. And I didn't come back."

"I knew it," Maria said. "That's *vile*—you know that, Whitelaw?"

"I'm not surprised," Jessica added. "I'm not surprised at all."

Desperately Devon turned to Ken. "You can understand I had to save myself, can't you, man? I had to save myself!"

Ken shook his head. "I would have done anything to save Olivia," he said softly. "Anything in the world. Your cowardice just makes me sick."

Devon looked around at the others in the crowd that had gathered. He searched the eyes of Winston Egbert, Maria Santelli, Aaron Dallas, and others he didn't know by name, hoping to see some glimmer of sympathy or understanding for what he'd done. But he saw nothing but disgust in their eyes.

His only hope was Elizabeth. She hadn't said anything, and he knew that she had truly loved him—more than any girl he'd ever known. Maybe, just maybe, she would understand . . . and be able to forgive him.

He glanced at her. She was staring at him with a galaxy of sadness in her eyes. Gathering his courage, he forced himself to meet her gaze.

"Elizabeth," he said. "You understand, don't you? I was frightened out of my mind. I was so scared, I couldn't even think straight."

Elizabeth didn't reply, but the sadness in her expression changed to pity.

"Please try to understand," he begged her, feeling more vulnerable than he'd ever felt in his life. "I was *terrified*. Is that a crime?"

"No," Elizabeth replied, looking away from Devon's beseeching gaze. "It's not a crime. But what's completely disgusting is the fact that you've been lying to us all this time."

Devon's hands fell open at his sides, and Elizabeth knew she had wounded him deep in his heart. She just couldn't bring herself to be sorry, though—not after the awful things he'd done.

"*Everyone* was terrified during the earthquake," Elizabeth continued. "But at least we tried to save our friends. You're a coward and a liar, Devon. How do you live with yourself?"

Devon's head drooped as she spoke. For a second she wondered if she was being too harsh. *No, she told herself, no, he deserves to hear the ugly truth. He deserves it more than anyone I've ever known.*

"And I never want to speak to you again as long as I live," Elizabeth told him. She stepped out of his way.

Devon raised his head and stared at her with horrible realization in his eyes. Elizabeth made herself hold his stare, letting him know that she'd meant every word she'd said.

Finally Devon nodded sadly and turned to leave.

As she watched him walk through the gate Elizabeth felt crushed with memories—of all the hopes she'd had for Devon, all the wonderful, romantic moments they'd shared. A part of her heart felt as if it were being torn away as she stared after his defeated figure. Devon had been the perfect guy for her—his intensity, sensitivity, and intelligent point of view had often meshed amazingly well with her own. And moments like the time they'd kissed in the field behind the school would always remain seared into her memory with a sizzling, passionate heat.

But he'd ruined it all with his deceit.

Now that I know what he really is, Elizabeth realized, *I can't feel any disappointment to see him go.*

Elizabeth closed the gate and turned back toward her friends.

Good-bye, Devon, Elizabeth thought. *I hope I never see you again.*

So this is it, Devon thought as he walked stiffly toward his motorcycle, which he'd parked at the curb outside the Davidsons' house. *This is how it ends.*

Now that he knew what everyone in Sweet Valley really thought of him, he could see no reason to stay. As soon as he could, he was going to hit the road and find another home.

Maybe Nan will come with me, Devon thought as he fired up his motorcycle. *Maybe the two of us can find someplace new to start again.*

Devon started down the street, heading toward home. The bright California sunlight warmed his back as broken palm trees swayed up ahead of him. Devon glared at the cute little houses on the way, some of which were already being repaired. *Sweet Valley,* he thought bitterly, *the most perfect place on earth.*

At the corner Devon turned, buzzing right through a red light. Up ahead was the school at which he'd first met Elizabeth—the school he wouldn't be returning to in the fall.

I was never happy here, he told himself as he drove. *This little town was always too nice for me—totally not my style. In fact, I'm glad so much of it got busted up in the earthquake. At least I'm leaving Sweet Valley in ruins.*

But as he drove past Sweet Valley High a sudden

wave of crushing sadness engulfed him. Devon had to pull over to keep from wiping out.

Stop lying, he told himself harshly. *You've lied to everyone else; don't lie to yourself too.*

He sat on his idling bike, staring up at the school. *You were a coward,* he told himself, *and you're just going to have to live with that.*

And yes, he would miss Sweet Valley terribly. He'd loved the school, where he'd been allowed to set his own pace and choose classes that had actually challenged him. His classmates had been friendly and welcoming, and he'd miss most of them very much.

Sweet Valley had been the first place he'd ever let himself call home. He'd loved this town . . . and one girl here in particular.

And I ruined my happiness. I lost it all, by being a spineless liar.

That was a horrible thing to realize about himself, but there was no way for Devon to deny that it was true. He'd loved Elizabeth Wakefield, and he'd abandoned her. He'd turned his back on the entire town and rejected all the happiness that had once been his.

Devon let himself cry as he started down the road again. Hot tears burned his eyes, and he blinked rapidly, feeling more miserable than he ever had in his life.

Good-bye, Sweet Valley, Devon thought as he revved his bike. *It's been real.*

But Devon Whitelaw is never coming back.

Chapter 15

"That was so cool, Lizzie," Jessica told her twin on their way back to Fowler Crest. "You were incredible. Man, it was so good to see that smug smirk wiped off Devon's face! You really let him have it."

"I don't know," Elizabeth replied as she steered the newly repaired Jeep. "I don't think we should be *gloating* about it, Jess. It was still a pretty awful experience."

"Please," Jessica countered. "You can't tell me Devon didn't deserve every word you said!"

"No, I guess not," Elizabeth said with a small smile. "He did have it coming."

"In a big way."

Jessica was furious at Devon and glad to see her twin was finally enjoying her revenge. *I nearly died trying to save Alyssa,* Jessica thought, *and I didn't even know her. Devon supposedly loved Liz, but he didn't try to save her at all! There's nothing worse than that.*

At the thought of Alyssa, Jessica grew more somber. There had been so much death and sadness lately, no wonder her rage at Devon had gotten her so excited. It felt wonderful to feel something else for a change.

Jessica settled back into the passenger seat of the freshly repaired Jeep, thinking back to Olivia's memorial service. Now *that* had been an emotional blowout. Even though she was still mad at Ken for how brutally he'd spoken to her that night they'd met in the SVH bleachers, Jessica wasn't about to deny that his speech had affected her deeply. Sometime during the middle of it Jessica had burst into tears and run to find Elizabeth.

As she hugged her sister, something deep within Jessica finally settled. The openhearted, brave way Ken had spoken about accepting Olivia's death had helped her realize—and finally *believe*—that there was nothing she could have done to save Alyssa.

Jessica had so much to live for too. She had the love of her family and friends—and she'd never underestimate the worth of that again.

Still, Jessica knew she'd never fully heal after watching Alyssa tumble down that fissure. She flinched at the thought—the pain of Alyssa's death would always be with her, just below the surface.

Maybe I didn't kill Alyssa, Jessica thought as

Elizabeth turned into the Fowlers' seemingly endless driveway. *But something inside me has died—and I won't be able to figure it all out for a long, long time. The Jessica I used to be will never live again.*

"What're you thinkin'?" Elizabeth asked as she pulled the Jeep up in front of the mansion.

"It's too much to explain," Jessica replied. "But I think I'm gonna be OK."

Elizabeth nodded, and both the twins got out of the Jeep. Hand in hand, they entered Fowler Crest—their new home for now.

Lucinda greeted them in the foyer. "There was a delivery for you, Miss Jessica," Lucinda said. "It's waiting on the hall table."

Jessica glanced at Elizabeth, who just shrugged. Together they walked out into the hall to see what had arrived.

"Roses," Jessica breathed as she hurried toward a huge bouquet on the giant oak table that dominated the front hall.

Elizabeth sniffed the robust red blossoms and smiled. "Who are they from?"

"I have no idea," Jessica replied, admiring the bouquet.

Elizabeth rolled her eyes. "Well, read the card, silly," she said.

Jessica quickly located a tiny envelope tucked into the flowers and ripped it open. It was from Marcus Pontil and his father, and the card read simply, *People like you give us hope.*

With a big smile, Jessica handed the card over for Elizabeth to read. And suddenly she realized she felt happy for the first time since the moment the earthquake had struck.

That was so sweet, Jessica thought, inhaling the wonderful smell of the roses.

Maybe it was finally time to look forward to the future.

Later that evening Todd stuffed a pair of nylon shorts into his new duffel bag. He was trying to pack for camp since he was leaving early the next morning for North Carolina. But all evening he hadn't been able to stop thinking about Elizabeth. What if she'd heard about him and Lila? Maybe he should call her and explain. . . . No. They'd decided to take a break for the summer, and he was going to stick to that plan. Besides, all the feelings he'd had about Lila in the past few days had left him confused and not a little bit embarrassed.

Todd realized that he was standing still, holding a pair of rolled-up socks in his hand. He shook his head as he packed the socks in the duffel bag.

"I'm really losing it," he said, rolling his eyes.

Behind him a young female voice said his name. Todd jumped, startled, and turned around.

Elizabeth stepped into his bedroom, an unsure smile on her face. "Hi, Todd," she said. "Is this a bad time?"

Todd blushed. "Hi, Liz," he replied. His heart

broke at the sight of her, so he turned back to his packing. "This is as good a time as any, I guess. What's going on?"

"Your mother said I could come up," Elizabeth said. "I hope that's OK."

"That's fine," Todd said. "I'm just packing. I'm leaving tomorrow."

"That's why I'm here," she said, her voice barely a whisper.

Todd froze. "To make sure I left town?" he asked sharply. Until that moment he hadn't realized how truly angry he still was.

Elizabeth was silent for a moment, and he felt a little guilty for his remark. But she'd hurt him badly, and she was just going to have to deal with his anger.

"Todd," Elizabeth said softly. "Don't be like that, OK? I just stopped by . . . to see if you wanted to talk."

Todd turned around to face her. "Do we have anything to talk about?" he asked, knowing all too well that they did.

"Well," Elizabeth began nervously, "we could talk about us. Where we stand now. I'd like to talk about that. Everything feels so . . . unfinished, you know what I mean?"

"I thought we decided to take a break—to talk about this when I get back," Todd replied.

"OK. If that's what you really want," she said, her voice strained. She started to leave. "I hope you have a great summer."

"Liz, wait." Todd grabbed her hand and she turned to him, tears shining in her beautiful blue-green eyes. A tiny voice in Todd's mind warned him that he would regret what he was about to do, but he couldn't help himself. He suddenly realized that all his longing for Lila, all his thoughts about kissing her, were completely misplaced. Elizabeth was the one he wanted—the only one he could ever want.

He pulled her to him and held her close, feeling her heart pounding against his chest.

"Oh, Todd," she sobbed quietly. "I'm so sorry for everything. I never wanted to hurt you."

Todd squeezed her tightly, afraid to speak. The emotions coursing through him were too over-whelming. All he could think about was how right she felt in his arms. How perfect and pure and sweet. "It's OK," Todd said quietly. "I know."

Elizabeth finally pulled away and blinked up at him.

"Close your eyes," Todd said. She did, and he slowly kissed each of her eyelids. "No more crying," he said. "Everything's going to be fine."

Elizabeth smiled weakly. "But not between us, right?" she asked. "I've pretty much guaranteed that."

It took all Todd's willpower to keep from kissing her for real. "I just don't know, Liz. I don't know if there'll ever be trust between us again."

Elizabeth nodded, obviously holding back tears.

"But I will miss you," Todd choked out. "I want

you to know that, Elizabeth. You're my best friend, and I'll never forget it."

Elizabeth took a deep breath. "Thank you for saying that, Todd. I'll miss you too."

She reached out and squeezed his hand, then started to back away. Todd held on to her, arguing with himself over whether or not to let her fingers slip from his grasp. Something inside told him that if he let her go now, he'd never hold her in his arms again.

Elizabeth stared at their entwined fingers. "I'd better go," she said.

Todd released her and stared at the place where their hands had been. "Yeah, you'd better. Good-bye, Elizabeth." Todd's heart had never felt so hollow.

"Good-bye," she said. And then she was gone.

At sunrise the next morning Elizabeth stepped out onto the sand of Crescent Beach. Jessica was by her side. The twins headed down toward the shoreline, where Elizabeth could see that a large group of her friends had already gathered for the scattering of Olivia's ashes.

The horizon was turning a pale yellow streaked with washes of a rosy pink as Elizabeth and Jessica joined the others in a wide semicircle around Mr. and Mrs. Davidson and Ken. All of Olivia's closest friends were present, as well as just about everyone Elizabeth knew from Sweet Valley High. Glancing around her, Elizabeth quickly spotted Enid, both Marias, Winston Egbert, Bruce Patman, and Jeffery French, along with everyone who had spoken at Olivia's memorial service. They all looked rumpled, sleepy, and sad, and Elizabeth felt the same way.

It's been such a difficult few days, Elizabeth thought as she exchanged sorrowful smiles with her friends. *Everything I've ever counted on has changed.*

Elizabeth searched the crowd for Todd and spotted him standing slightly behind her in the arc of the circle. Part of her wanted to go to him. She craved his strength. But they'd said their goodbyes last night, and there was no need to prolong the inevitable. *Todd is leaving*, she thought. *He was the most stable thing in my life for ages, but now even he's moving on, with not much promise for our future together.*

And Devon . . . She was pleased to notice that he hadn't dared to show his face there this morning. If only he would keep up his disappearing act forever, Elizabeth would be entirely glad.

What a relief it is to have my memories back! Elizabeth thought. She hadn't felt complete without them—and look how easy it had been for Devon to fool her when she hadn't been able to look back at a part of her own past.

There was still only one mystery left to be solved. Elizabeth still didn't know the identity of

the mysterious stranger who had saved her and
Enid. Ken had been the only person to see him,
and he hadn't gotten a good look at his face. *I'm
sure he'll come forward and reveal himself in time,*
Elizabeth thought. *Or at least I hope he does. It
would be nice to thank him for saving my life!*

"Please, everyone, take each other's hands,"
Mrs. Davidson said. She was wearing a long, flow-
ing white dress decorated with small batiks of but-
terflies, and she was holding a copper urn in her
hands. "We'll get started in a moment. I'm just
going to wait a few more minutes for any stragglers
to arrive."

Elizabeth took Jessica's hand on one side and
Enid's on the other side. The group was silent as
they waited for the Davidsons to begin, and the
only sounds were the restless lapping of the ocean
against the sand and the occasional cry of a
seabird.

Jessica gave Elizabeth's hand a little squeeze,
and Elizabeth turned to smile at her twin. *She
seems so much better,* Elizabeth decided. *But is she
really? How can anyone ever really get over what
Jessica has lived through?*

Deep below Jessica's surface placidity, Elizabeth
knew, was still a lot of unresolved pain. It would
take a long time for Jessica to heal—if she ever
really recovered completely.

With a sigh Elizabeth looked around the semicircle again, feeling warmed by the sight of all the

familiar faces. *I love so many of these people,* she realized. *This is what Sweet Valley really is—not the buildings themselves. Sweet Valley is made up of all the people I love and who love me in return.*

Together they would all rebuild the town. It wouldn't be easy, that was for sure. So many things had been destroyed. The town might change forever, but the love would remain the same.

"Thank you all for coming here this morning," Mrs. Davidson told the assembled group of Olivia's friends. "I'm going to make this quick and simple, as we all said our good-byes to Olivia yesterday." She held up the urn and showed it to the semicircle. "These are Olivia's ashes," she said. "We chose this spot to scatter them because more than anyplace else, Olivia loved the ocean, especially this stretch of beach right here where we're standing.

"This is where she'd come to paint. This is where she'd come to walk, to lose herself in the beauty of nature for a little while. And her father and I could not think of a better spot for her to join nature for all eternity."

With those words Mrs. Davidson opened the urn. Mr. Davidson and Ken both stepped forward and reached their hands into the large opening. After they'd each withdrawn a handful of ashes, they stepped back.

Elizabeth took a deep breath as Mrs. Davidson started shaking the remainder of the ashes into the air, where they surrounded her in a thick cloud for a moment before dissipating, drifting in every direction. Mr. Davidson and Ken released their handfuls into the wind. The little gray specks of what used to be Olivia's body floated into the sky, some raining down into the water, some falling onto the sand, and some drifting over the semicircle of Olivia's friends who had come to say good-bye.

Elizabeth closed her eyes as the ashes fell, tightly gripping Jessica and Enid's hands in her own.

Farewell, Olivia, Elizabeth whispered in her mind. *I will never forget you.*

I feel so different, Jessica thought as she watched Olivia's ashes drift over the greenish blue Pacific Ocean. So many things had happened to her in the days since her birthday, both wonderful miracles and terrible tragedies. *It's changed me,* she realized. *So much so that I'm not even sure who I am anymore.*

Ken turned to face the group with a deeply sorrowful expression on his face. It wasn't the hopeless misery Jessica had seen that night in the SVH bleachers—Ken was no longer killing himself by drowning in a mire of guilt and despair. *Is that what I look like?* Jessica wondered. *We've both come so far since that awful night.* No longer was she constantly attacking herself for her role in Alyssa's death, but she also felt profoundly saddened to her core.

"We all need to look to the future," Ken called out. "I've learned I can do that with Olivia's love still intact in my heart, and so can all of you."

I'm ready to face the future too, Jessica realized. *But as who?*

She knew she couldn't be the crazy, wild, care-free girl she'd been all through her junior year of high school. That girl died along with Alyssa Hewitt.

The new Jessica had a heavy seriousness weighing down her soul—a seriousness that still made her feel very uncomfortable with herself. It was incredibly difficult, this metamorphosis into someone new, into someone who could handle the terrible sadness that had forever lodged in her heart. But Jessica knew that she had to struggle on because the alternative was unthinkable—it was only ashes scattered to the wind.

Mr. Davidson took the urn from his wife and closed it. He hugged his wife and pulled Ken in with their embrace too. Mrs. Davidson pulled away for a second and opened her arms to the group, inviting them all in.

Jessica stepped forward to be held—and to hold—in the giant group hug. After a long moment of pressing tightly against their friends, they started to move apart again. And as the group shifted around her, suddenly Jessica found herself face-to-face with Ken.

"Have you forgiven yourself?" she asked him.

He nodded. "Mostly," he replied softly. "How about you?"

"Yes," Jessica said. "I think I really have."

Ken pulled Jessica to him, wrapping his lean, muscular arms around her. "I'm sorry for freaking out on you the other night," he whispered. "I was . . . well, I was pretty messed up."

"I understand," Jessica told him. "I'm sorry too, for being so insensitive."

Ken smiled at her, and then he was pulled away, back into the group.

With a sigh Jessica turned around to find Elizabeth and Lila standing behind her. She clasped hands with her twin and threw her free arm around Lila's shoulders. "You guys about ready to head back home?" she asked.

"I'm ready," Elizabeth replied.

"Let's go," Lila said. "I heard that our new chef is a whiz at breakfast."

As the three of them headed up the beach toward the Jeep, Jessica smiled.

At least I still have my friends and family, she thought, *if they can learn to accept the new me.*

Whoever she was becoming, there was one thing Jessica knew for sure. Sweet Valley would never be the same again.

It's a new beginning with a lot of attitude. Don't miss SVH Senior Year #1: **Can't Stay Away***, coming to bookstores in January 1999. Senior Year: It's about love. It's about life. It's about time.*

Bantam Books in the Sweet Valley High series
Ask your bookseller for the books you have missed

Surf's Up at Sweet Valley

Francine Pascal's
SWEET VALLEY

Sneak Peeks
Hot News
Meet Francine Pascal
Mailing List
Bookshelf

Check out **Sweet Valley Online** when you're surfing the Internet!
It is *the* place to get the scoop on what's happening with your
favorite twins, Jessica and Elizabeth Wakefield, and the gang at
Sweet Valley. The official site features:

Sneak Peeks
Be the first to know all the juicy details of upcoming books!

Hot News
All the latest and greatest Sweet Valley news including
special promotions and contests.

Meet Francine Pascal
Find out about Sweet Valley's creator and send her a letter by e-mail!

Mailing List
Sign up for Sweet Valley e-mail updates and give us your feedback!

Bookshelf
A handy reference to the World of Sweet Valley.

★ ★

Check out Sweet Valley Online today!

http://www.sweetvalley.com

BFYR 145